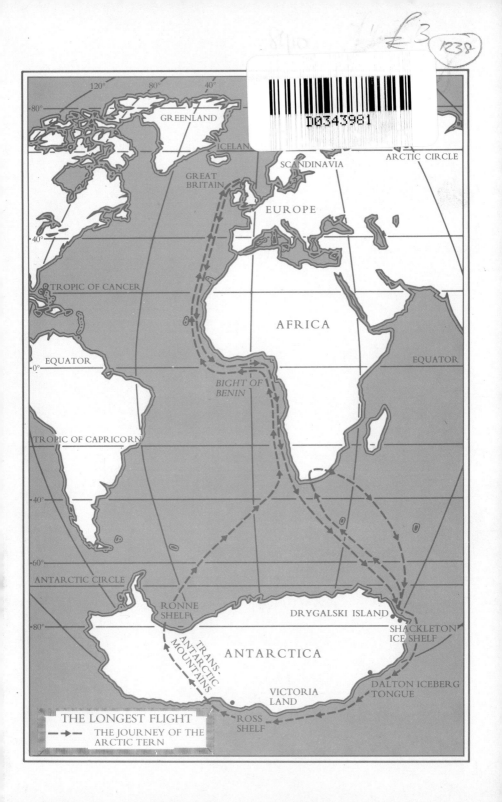

THE LONGEST FLIGHT

THE JOURNEY OF THE
ARCTIC TERN

The
Longest
Flight

by the same author

WHALE

JEREMY LUCAS

The Longest Flight

JONATHAN CAPE
THIRTY BEDFORD SQUARE LONDON

First published in Great Britain 1982
copyright © 1982 by Jeremy Lucas
Jonathan Cape Ltd, 30 Bedford Square, London WC1

British Library Cataloguing in Publication Data

Lucas, Jeremy
The longest flight.
I. Title
813'.54 [F]   PS3562.U236

ISBN 0-224-01960-0

Printed in Great Britain by
Butler & Tanner Ltd,
Frome and London

For those who travel to Northern Scotland
and find themselves possessed by what lies there,
and for those in whose hands its destiny
is held

Contents

Preface

Man and wild beast have long shared a destiny, a journey through evolution. Together we have seen the wonders of the world and have made more in our passing. The story of migration is one of those wonders.

As I write, the most northerly fresh-water loch on the British mainland stretches out before me and the sea is within hearing range beyond the river. A shoal of sea-trout is running on a high tide. The nets have not left many, neither has winter in the open Atlantic, but these few have come through and are beginning the next dangerous part of their migration to the breeding burns at the head of the loch.

This book, however, is the story of a different journey: the longest migration on earth, an adventure that twice spans half the globe in a single year. It is the story of the arctic tern, a wild sea-bird, his flight, his struggle against skuas and falcons and the spoiling of the ocean's face. It is as close to the truth as I can tell it. If it is dramatic, the tern itself has made it so.

Here, on Scotland's north-western rim, is a sprawling, broken shore, a land and a sea locked in constant battle. From the high moor between Altnaharra and Loch Loyal, west across peaty hills to the sea and down to the lochs and mountain mass of Ross, is the last wilderness of the mainland. And beyond, across the Minch, in the curl of a shattered comma, lie the outer isles. The Seven Hunters and St Kilda are the last of the land before the shelf drops and all is grey-blue for three thousand miles of restless Atlantic Ocean. It is here, before oil and the pressures of civilisation take too strong a grasp, that the tern's flight begins.

The events within this story are all possible; nothing is fantasy. It is entirely likely that the strange old common tern, whom I call Hawkwind, would accompany arctic terns rather than his own kind. In keeping with zoological fact, however, I have not allowed Hawkwind the extended migration to Antarctica. Skubill, the great skua, is one of an increasing number of predators which, indirectly aided by mankind, are causing havoc among breeding colonies of northern terns. Greyback, the magnificent wandering albatross, is a unique animal; but even he probably exists somewhere in the remoter regions of the south Atlantic. And James, the boy we meet in the *Firedragon* episode, lives in the heart of every boy who yearns for the freedom and beauty of the sea.

Long before the terns must leave, my own southern journey begins, a human migration for man-made needs; and yet in the vision of the loch and the hills there is a belief of return, and hope that the spell of rock and tide remains, as it must for other creatures which have travelled far from here.

Loch Hope, Sutherland
July 1981

J.L.

10

Note on the arctic tern

An adult arctic tern is fifteen inches long. It has a slender build with pointed, back-swept wings and deeply forked tail. It resembles a swallow in shape and is the size of a small hawk. In full breeding plumage it is white and pearl-grey with scarlet legs and bill. The top half of its head is capped with glossy black. Even experts have great difficulty in distinguishing between common and arctic terns and the sexes of both species are differentiated almost entirely by behaviour. The study of the arctic tern reveals something that has reached perfection in evolution and adaptation.

PART ONE

Sea-swallow

ONE

Hawkwind, a one-eyed common tern, had been a long time away from home. He was not visible from the surface of the sea above which he flew. His altitude was too great, his size too small. There had been few times in his life when he had not been one of many, when he had not belonged to the discipline of a flock, but now, after an exhausting flight from the Southern Ocean, he was alone. Being more than two decades old the desire for a female no longer bothered him. He ignored the calls of flock leaders, sloping clear whenever they approached and ascending beyond their vision. They always allowed the old tern to pass; they did not need him.

Water vapour was condensing on his shoulders, holding him back. Annoyed by his loss of momentum he pressed down more viciously. He shot out of dense cumulo-nimbus and found himself in thin, freezing air with only a few narrow wisps of cloud above him. A shower of ice splinters hushed across his wings and back, and clung there, white and silver in the sun. His lungs began to sting with the effort of fast breathing. He had spent two hours climbing from sea-level to an altitude of nearly ten thousand feet, and the lack of oxygen was making him light-headed.

As a fledgling Hawkwind had lost his left eye to a skua which had attacked him on the nest. Protected by his parents he had survived and adapted until his disability caused him little concern. He was smaller than most of his kind though tirelessly strong; he held his head in a slightly crooked way, for, with only one eye, navigation was a problem. Age had weakened his wings, but over the years he had built up an intimate knowledge of the coasts along his migratory path.

At last Hawkwind could climb no higher. With blood throbbing in his head he knew he had reached his ceiling. Beneath him there was no more cloud. Now he would plane comfortably, expending little energy. Turning his head to the left he brought the coast into the field of view of his good eye. He could see the thrashing white necklace upon every shore exposed to the west; and yet the Hebridean island strongholds remained fast against the Atlantic's endless surge and tumble. The heights of Ben Clisham and Tirga More on Lewis seemed barely to rise above the moorlands. The Sound of Harris stretched beneath him now, a fast swirl of currents licking across the shell-sand beaches of Pabbay and Berneray. Gradually he was dropping, while the intense blue of the Little Minch rolled ahead. Hearing the mounting wind buzzing through his frayed pinions he slanted towards the east. In an hour he had lost a mile of altitude, but still, as he beat across the Sound of Shiant into the North Minch, he knew he would arrive at his destination long before nightfall.

Once he reached the mainland the common tern cruised across the moorland south of Cape Wrath to meet the sea again at the Kyle of Durness. Here he did not need the navigational expertise of companions, for this was his home. Quietly now he rose and continued eastwards. The colours of the sky reflected from his journey-dulled feathers, a pale blue sheen, silvered at the edges.

Not far away, as the weary bird thrashed across the boundless sky on the last few miles of his migration, another life, which would soon become the downy form of a tern chick, was thrashing within the bounds of a warm shell.

TWO

The tide was never still. It whipped, heaved and foamed about the battered line of reefs at the cliff's base. The wind-borne spray hissed against bare granite forty feet clear of the tide-mark and ran, in a white sun-lit torrent, back into the sea. Herring gulls soared ceaselessly on the cliff's updraught, and screeched their high repeating calls while their alert eyes watched for unguarded nests, or pierced the clear water just beyond the reef.

Mosses and yellow lichens carpeted the storm-smoothed rock in those places where the salt did not reach or the birds did not tread. The cliff was etched with crevices and grassy ledges, and at its rounded heather-clad summit, it stood three hundred feet above the angry Atlantic.

Just beyond the reach of the roaring waves was a small colony of common terns, and higher, on a nest of wrack and grass and rock, sat Nightwing, a female arctic tern. Continuously her head turned skywards, her stare upon the annoying shapes of the circling gulls. Beneath her belly nestled a single egg, warm despite the stone on which it lay. At dawn, while the dew still hung to her breast, Nightwing had felt a mounting stir within the shell. She had felt the embryo's egg-tooth scratching and probing. She had spoken to ears within the egg which would hear and be comforted, a being which would be spurred on by her reassuring voice.

A fork-tailed smudge moved across the sky, slowed to a hover, and hung, translucent against the mid-morning sun. A strident high-pitched call cut the air, 'keerree', and with wings held up the bird plummeted towards the gulls. They banked and dispersed, giving the falling flash a clear passage to the nest. Two curving wings shot out, beating the air and slowing the stoop. The flash became the sleek pale shape of Shocksilver, Nightwing's mate. For a few moments he glided, flicking his head from side to side, while he made sure that it was safe to land. Then he was at the female's side, listening to her welcoming 'kik, kik' noises, and nodding his head to reassure her after his long absence. He had been gone since dawn, hunting and dipping upon the sea, gliding across the swelling acres, with the shadowy hump of Sutherland at his tail. Now he had returned so that Nightwing could hunt in the flowing tide, while he replaced her upon their egg and guarded the nest.

Three minutes later, a mile from the cliff colony, Nightwing soared above the shallows of Auk Island. The high June sun played with the ripples, and cast shining patterns over the weed-flecked sands. The tern's fleet wings, angular and crescent shaped, worked in the buffeting breeze that kicked up from the surface beneath her. She rose thirty feet into the air, until a movement behind the surf caused her to pause, and hang, kestrel-like, while her quick brain analysed her target. In a moment a sand-eel lay dead in her beak, its life blasted away in a shower of spray and foam. Again she rose, soared away from the breakers, and came to rest upon the sea a hundred yards from the beach.

Back on the nest Shocksilver was watching his mate. The egg beneath him vibrated, and from time to time he felt a slight tapping. Eighteen years earlier Shocksilver had hatched close to where he now lay. Sixteen times he had made the long migration of his kind, and sixteen times he had returned from the southern hemisphere to this same Scottish cliff. He had returned each time with Nightwing, whom he had met upon the Antarctic ice-shelf. They had crossed the trackless sea, following only their instincts and their memories of earlier journeys.

For a month now they had been home. At first they had been two specks against the chasm of a May sky; flicking and criss-crossing high in the air; joining, breaking apart and falling seaward to swoop, stretch-winged precious inches above the crests.

Now, in the blustering babble of life in the North Atlantic summer, the two birds took it in turns to fish and to sit the nest. At night they nuzzled up close to one another with their heads turned together and touching, and their egg safe between them. At first light each day Shocksilver lifted his wings and slipped silently into the wind. For a mile he would beat landward across the heather moor to a still-surfaced loch where trout and salmon par rose, vulnerable to the tern's lethal dive. As the sun burst between the great mountain masses of Hope and Loyal, Shocksilver would swing towards the sea, to spend the morning fishing and playing upon the turbulent reach of water between Auk Island and the cliff.

Nightwing spent less time away from the nest than her mate, although the instinct of protection was strong in both birds. The sharp-eyed gulls worried her, for if both she and Shocksilver left the nest for long their egg would be devoured before their return. Shocksilver's vigilance was unfailing, and yet, this time, after less than an hour's fishing, Nightwing sped across the shallows as she moved homeward.

In this place, upon the moorland edge of the British Isles, there were few men. The cliffs stood, whittled and worn by the tides of ages, in tune with eternal geological pace. The animals that came with each changing season did little more than add character and living motion to a cold backdrop of rock and sea.

Here, above the reaching talons of spray, the terns made their bid for survival and the perpetuation of their kind.

THREE

The rapidly waning crescent fell sunward, drifted a moment upon the orange curve of the horizon, and then dissolved against the dusk-burnished ocean. Nightwing, upon the nest, watched and waited for the crescent to reappear and grow, until it became the fast-flying shape of Shocksilver returning to her side.

The shadows cast by the June day deepened, so that while she was still, Nightwing was invisible against the rock. Here and there eye-catching flickers of movement betrayed the bird colonies, though now the tide's voice was far louder than those of the arguing gulls or the territory-conscious gannets. Across the race of turbulent water, Auk Island lay like a great stranded sea-giant; silent and asleep, upon the summer-soft tide.

Beneath her, Nightwing felt a crack. She stood and looked down upon the pale, brown-flecked egg. A jagged split from end to end had formed and the egg rocked gently in obedience to the welling, confused strength within its limits. Nightwing glanced about her. High above, with belly singed gold against the sun's last rays, a buzzard soared in a wide sweeping spiral. Towards the sea two black-backed gulls floated behind the island and did not reappear. She called out 'kee', shrill and far-reaching. Then she looked back at the egg and waited.

Three terns appeared a long way off. Behind and above them, on blurred thrusting wings, Shocksilver dropped, called as he closed with his destination.

Long before the common terns reached the cliff, Nightwing heard the sudden rush and flutter of air that preceded her mate's careful landing. Few eyes were fast enough to have seen his return, and now, in the purpling shadow of the cliff, none could see the motionless forms of the two arctic terns, as each stood, side by side, watching a small shining bill probing into the air from the fragmenting egg.

There in the fading light the spirit of the mother cliff was strong, protecting the birds and bringing peace for the short summer night. The arctic tern chick, a glistening heap of tiny movements, struggled to right himself until the floor of his nest lay beneath his feet.

At first he was a sticky ball of down, shivering as the cool night air rushed into his lungs. He fell as he tried to stand, and was afraid of the ocean's murmur about the cliff. To soothe him were two warm shapes with their low 'kik, kik' sounds, and gently stroking beaks searching his down, removing the clammy vestiges of the egg.

By dawn the wind had dried him into a fluffy brown-blotched ball, nestling beneath the warm comfort of Nightwing's breast. The continuity of the wave sounds were now almost as reassuring as his mother's voice, and the first light of day did not dazzle him, but came as a welcoming warmth upon his downy feathers.

Three times Shocksilver's call resounded about the cliff. Soon, in the velvet half-light, he was poised above the reef, screeching warnings to all those who might

23

otherwise dare approach the nest. Then he allowed the wind to lift him, vertically, until his body flared against the radiance of the morning sun.

It was then that Hawkwind appeared, having spent a night roosting on Auk Island. The eyes of a hundred nesting birds turned seaward to watch the new arrival with his slightly awkward flight, his crooked neck. Nightwing immediately recognised the old tern, for on each one of previous nesting years Hawkwind and his female had made a scrape close to Nightwing's own. They had been breeding neighbours. The flat mounds at the cliff's base belonged as much to Hawkwind as to the arctics. There was a quick glow of contented excitement within her as Nightwing recognised her old companion, but soon it dimmed, for now she possessed a greater contentment, rustling and fluffy-warm beneath her breast. At a glance she observed that Hawkwind was alone this time; the great migration had been cruel that year.

Shocksilver curled and whipped past Hawkwind's tail. The two friends together bowed their wings and allowed the sea-draught to throw them across the sky. They chattered and sang their slightly different calls which both birds understood, since they meant the same thing. They aimed themselves towards the coastal mountains and then stooped until they were rushing across heather moor. They hugged the contours they both knew so well, alert and watchful for those birds into whose territory they briefly encroached.

A harrier, upon an early hunt, saw the terns' speeding forms and swerved to follow. A pair of grouse, startled by the sudden rush of air, lurched from their hollow. On madly flapping wings they bolted half a mile downwind, shattering the peace of the moorland with their angry voices: 'go-back, go-back, go-back'. The harrier veered and gave chase, the difficult target of the terns forgotten.

Shocksilver had seen the hawk's shape lagging far behind, and, followed by Hawkwind, he dropped in a long hissing dive across stony ground, until the waters of the loch stretched beneath him: comforting and open. On the windward shore the surface was ruffled. The terns could see little until they came to the calmer bays along the lee shore.

They soared, almost motionless, above a line of birch trees. Sea-trout fry and brown-trout formed expanding rings on the surface as they rose to a morning hatch of olive dun. The sea-trout, shy and fast, saw a flicker of the terns' wings and dived beneath rocks and weed. Some bolted for deeper water while brown-trout, less sensitive and not so fearful as their ocean-migrating brethren, continued moving upon the surface, mopping up flies with their slow porpoise-like roll. The terns hung, as poised as kestrels, waiting for the right moment to attack.

A ring spread in the shallows, and then another a foot beyond the first. Shocksilver was already moving as the fish surfaced for the third time. With wings delicately turned up he descended along the trout's line of travel. In the last moment his head lunged down so that his bill cut beneath the water. At forty miles per hour he reached skyward. Beneath him now was a dash of foam upon the still waters, and nothing more to mark his kill save a temporary absence of surfacing fish. Sideways in his bill lay a three-inch trout.

A shoal of yearling sea-trout moved sixty yards downwind. Their bodies twinkled slightly as they chased dun nymphs. The tiny movement caught Hawkwind's keen vigil. He slid from his poise and descended until he was gliding mere inches above the loch's crinkled surface. In front of the shoal his tail came round, turning him over, and his wings became flush with his body. A thin column of spray shot three feet above him while his bill lanced sideways towards a sea-trout's bright flank. Before the spray had settled the shoal had dispersed, and Hawkwind had reappeared with the glinting prize held firmly in his bill. For a minute he swam, until he saw Shocksilver's shape gliding above him. He thrust his feet down, tilted his wings into the wind, and burst into the air. Side by side, each bearing his own fish, the two terns beat away from the loch and made for the cloudless blue gash of the ocean beyond the heather moor.

Eyes glowing with diamonds of greed, gulls waited above the cliff. Nightwing had been watching them anxiously since the common tern and her mate had left. Now the scavenger birds had noticed the trout borne by the returning terns. Shocksilver and Hawkwind found themselves mobbed, surrounded by driving wings and slashing bills. They were disorientated, a rain of raucous killer-screams in their ears.

Then Nightwing was in the sky, shouting her own fury as she drove towards the males. The shoulder of her right wing clipped a gull's head, sending it spiralling in ruffled retreat. The scavengers heard the danger note in the brood-female's voice and retreated, greed dulled in frightened eyes. Soon the terns were alone upon their ledge. In a moment Nightwing had taken Shocksilver's trout and gulped it down, while Hawkwind, his head turned so that he held the downling in his stare, dropped his own fish at the female's feet. He had done this a thousand times before with his own mate; but she was

26

gone now and his own desire for food had lessened. Nightwing's need, and that of her downling, was greater. With a stab the female had removed the trout from the rock, turning it over once before dropping it head first into her chick's questing bill. Instantly it was gone and the tiny bill reopened, reaching towards Nightwing, empty of food and full of hope.

FOUR

With an ocean anticyclone passing slowly over the northern British Isles, the weather held. The sea was calm, so that nesting birds found fishing easy in the clear waters. They had only to cruise a hundred feet above the ground-swell and wait for the flash-edged shadows of a shoal of fish to drift into view. The cormorants, shags and auks found the fish in this way and then settled upon the sea, padding quietly, waiting for the fish to show beneath them. A quick bar of light flashed, far down in the blue and they flung themselves over, converting their wings into swift-stroking flippers, and thrust themselves in pursuit. The gulls, gannets and terns were not so patient. They could all swim, but did so more to rest than to watch the deep. They killed from the sky, diving upon the shoals at the instant of sight. Singly, or in great flocks, they dropped upon the sea's abundance.

The terns fished without the noisy company of the masses. They stalked their prey, singling out the fish of the right size, covering many miles of ocean or loch in a single day. They were the falcons of the shore; lightning smears of motion above the white smother of the sea upon a distant reef.

On the grassy sweep of rock lower down the cliff than Nightwing's nest the chicks of the common terns had hatched about the same time as their arctic cousin. Most of the nests were filled with two or three downlings. Without competition from brothers or sisters the young arctic was growing rapidly, and within three weeks his down had become smooth, brown-patterned feathers. Already he was becoming the sleek shape of the adults, though their colours and their skills would take far longer to attain.

Quickly the downling became attuned to the sights and sounds of his home. When a shadow passed over the nest he slunk down beneath his parent's wing, and if the shadow remained too long he knew how to use his fierce language to dissuade a potential predator. 'Kee-kee, kee, kee', he spat at the gulls, mimicking his mother, as each displayed the gaping red gash of a bill, and spread the twinned machete of their wings.

Each day the young tern walked farther from his nest. The limits of the ledge and his parents' calls stopped him from travelling beyond. They fed him thirty meals a day; with sprat, eel or trout, with caddis and butterfly, shrimp and ragworm, and once with the flesh of squid. No creature, with the exception of Hawkwind, was ever allowed to approach him. The pitted skull of a rat lay nearby as evidence of the tern's protective ferocity. An otter which had climbed from the broiling foam of high tide, to rest upon the ledge, had been mobbed and sent, with a yicker of fear, back into the sea.

For the time being it was enough for the downling to be able to sit upon the ledge's seaward edge, with the wind plucking at his sprawl of feathers, and the Atlantic heaving beneath. Day-long he fed and watched the

29

winged acrobats soar and swoop before him. Until the desire for free flight upon the cliff's air-flows overcame his awe, it would be enough merely to watch; but in the way of his kind he would not have long to wait.

FIVE

Upon the highest ramparts of the cliff, and on the moor beyond, were the nests of the sea-scavengers. Mainly they were arctic and pomerine skuas, though within an hour's flight of the tern colony there were three pairs of great skuas. Among the birds of the North-Western Isles these were the most hated. They were feared more than falcons, more persistent in their piratical ways than gulls, and they were merciless in their killing. Theirs was a reign of winged terror.

The most despised of all their race was Skubill. In the heather he had a mate and two fat fledglings. To feed them he killed anything that could be mastered by his heavy, two-foot length. He robbed the sea-birds of their meals by chasing them, hawklike, until they dropped or disgorged their burden. Tirelessly he outflew his victims, dropping down upon them, or sweeping up from beneath, slicing with the great hook of his bill. If they carried no food he took them instead. Rats and squirrels, grouse, divers, gulls and gannets, all fell beneath his strength. He had even killed an adult male black-back who had dared to defy him. The chicks of the sea-birds were his favourite prey, and so the breeding grounds of

Scotland were his kingdom. Even the falcons feared Skubill, for they had learnt long ago that their talons were almost useless against the pirate's cunning.

On the days when his kills upon the peat moor did not satisfy the greed of his family, the great skua flew, glint-eyed, above the colony cliff. While the birds sped for the sanctuary of their nests, he soared above the heaving waters towards Auk Island. Minutes after his arrival, instead of a thousand wings flapping carelessly on the air-stream, there would be a cacophony of rebellious, fearful voices, all focussed upon Skubill's dark shape. Impervious to their hatred, he would rise from the island and begin his search for enticing nests.

As he approached the tern colony they flew at him; Shocksilver, Hawkwind and the common terns, bursting from the cliff face, screeching and furious. Two by two they came at him, tilting in the last moment in an attempt to strike him with their wings as they passed. Skubill barked at them, 'Tuk-ray, tuk, tuk-ray', and snapped at their wings as they shot past; but while he was alone he could not break through a defence as determined as that of the terns.

The dark shape rose steeply away from the halo of white birds, and climbed until it was well clear of their colony and their anger. Like a buzzard, Skubill circled until the nests of the kittiwakes, upon exposed ledges towards the summit, caught his hungry stare. Again he closed with the cliff, turned sideways on, and swooped.

Far away the deafening cries of the sea-birds could be heard as the great skua began his carnage. The kittiwakes, unlike the terns, were not fierce in the defence of their young. They were dainty birds with neither the speed nor the spectacular courage of the tern races. Pathetically the adults fluttered above their nests, while Skubill crashed his beak through their eggs, or gulped down their chicks. He robbed six nests before he lofted his wings and thrust his laden weight into the air. Below him were the broken families, a sticky mess smeared over the stone, and shattered shells. He tilted away, falling in a lazy glide until he was almost skating upon the sea. Half a mile over the swell, he settled, with his head and tail cocked high, his attitude defiant, and already watchful for new sources of food.

In the northern dusk he returned, a dark sinew of form stroking low over the waves. Only the arctic downling, standing at the limits of the ledge as he watched the mobile pattern of the sea's dim shadows, saw him coming. Nightwing and Shocksilver sat well back from the edge, the female watching her chick, the male asleep. Hawkwind stood close by, his blind side turned to the sea. Peace smothered and seduced, and brought danger on silent wings.

Skubill crossed the reefs. He looked up and immediately saw the downling silhouetted against the gloaming. He adjusted his position on the slow evening airs so as to lift himself towards his target. The young tern continued to watch, entranced by the growing black shape, the flashing eyes, the great wings sweeping, the scratch marks on the skua's bill. Closer; a folding darkness, a realisation of danger, the skua's foul breath, a blow which sent the downling tumbling across the ledge. Skubill had made a mistake. He had meant to pluck his victim away from sanctuary, to finish him off away from the colony. Shadows and poor light had confused his aim. The downling was on his back, his feet held above his belly into two spread claws, his bill and wings open, the

33

epitome of defiance and defence. This Skubill saw in an instant as again he swooped; but it was nothing to him, nothing that his great beak could not master. And the sounds in the sky, of suddenly awakened birds, of startled terror, of defence calls and the spitting chick, were all as music to him.

Then Shocksilver's bill stabbed hard into Skubill's neck. Enraged, the skua swung round only to be thrown from the ledge by Hawkwind's full weight careering into his chest. Startled by the unexpected turn of events, Skubill parachuted his wings to regain stability. He rose with panicked wing beats while the terns tore at him, the air loaded with noise and hatred, and the sweeping silver swords of pinions.

Close to the shore of Auk Island, his initiative thwarted, Skubill sank to the sea. With dark walls of surging waves behind him he was difficult to attack. He raised his head and bellowed his killer cries at the terns, 'tuk, tuk, tuckay', but they had gone and his new-found courage was wasted on empty air.

The downling sat shivering beneath his mother's wing. Her gentle 'kik, kik, kik' was slowly forcing away the vision of the folding black shape, of fierce cries and violence out in the dusk. Although for his own sake he would never completely forget; he had learnt and he had been lucky. Skubill, the death-bird, was now part of the night, for the moment no more dangerous than the slumbering mid-summer sea.

SIX

The chick was no longer a downling. He had lost his irregular markings and fluffy appearence. His shape had assumed a swallow form, the size of a small hawk, though his colours, even in youth, told that he was a bird of the sea. Brown and buff specks patterned his head, neck and back. The shoulder of each wing was a light grey which stretched down to a darker shade along his primaries. A smudge of deep red coloured the point of his bill while the basal half was black. All else was white or a dusky grey. He had become a fledgling.

His world was his ledge and all that his sharp sight could behold of the ocean to the north. The facing walls of Auk Island, with its crowded nests and streaks of bird-lime, and the torture of waves, had held his attention for over three weeks so that he would never forget its detail. Now impatience, the precursor to adventure, coursed in his veins, baiting him, tempting him beyond the confines of the ledge. Often he had spread his wings to feel the brief lift which made him lose his balance and stumble back into the nest. Soon he learned to lean forwards as he opened his rapidly growing pinions, and to use slight movements to compensate for the fickle moods of the breeze. He no longer fell. Instead his heart raced whenever he felt the cool air plucking at his flight feathers, or when he watched the baffling aerobatics of the flight-masters, of fulmars and guillemots, that swooped and curled above the tide.

It was necessary to leave the cliff. The scavengers were becoming more dangerous and persistent. Skubill, his lesson learnt, would not be defeated again.

The fledgling stood above the sea while his parents fluttered before him. Nightwing turned and called out, 'kee', as she broke from her poise and cut away from the rock. He watched her, enthralled by her aerial display. Hawkwind was above, his voice tempting the young tern and banishing his moment of fear. The fledgling's wings were spread, his neck stretched; the sea gurgled and swept beneath, itself calling, enticing.

At low tide the water foamed forty feet below. Shock-silver dived from high above, screeching, 'kee, keeray', and curving away as his fledgling crouched, his trembling wings leaning against the ocean wind. Hawkwind's persistent calls from the sky were urgent, almost mocking the young tern for his reluctance to slip away from sanctuary. Nightwing came from below, bursting up from the white of seething waves, looping with her belly flashing before the young one's eyes. In that instant, in a disorientated blur of wings and rock, the fledgling reached forward into the air blast. He felt weightless as he rushed towards the surf, diving and picking up speed. His chest seemed wrenched apart. Then he was aware of a great roar of the reaching water inches beneath his tail. He did not see Nightwing at his side until long after he had met the first few buffeting shocks of air that spun from the peak of each wave. And it was not until he had turned up, reaching for the more comfortable currents above the sea's dizzying rush, that he heard Shocksilver and Hawkwind calling from high in the sky.

Within a minute his wings were confidently stroking him along. He rose towards the looming bulk of Auk Island. Ledges and crevices, and puffin burrows at the summit, grew in front of him; black rock closed around him like a skua's dark shape. His left wing dropped down and in a moment he was flat against the granite, skimming along the cliff. Then the wind caught his upraised right wing and carried him back out over the tide race. There before him, stood the cliff of his birth; and stretching away beyond, growing into large distant humps, were the mountains of Sutherland.

The fledgling was now flanked by the adults. His heart still raced; but the fear and reluctance were gone. He had only to turn up the leading edge of his wings and he was facing the empty blue void of the sky. In the moment of his brave lurch from the cliff-face he had infinitely increased the limits of his world. The ledge was nothing, a mere speck above the common tern colony. Even Auk Island could be approached, and left behind at his whim. Now the well of space above him and the sun-swept ocean were his. And already he felt the draw of their fathomless blue distance.

The line of reefs beneath the colony cliff lay uncovered by the low tide, carpeted in wrack, brown and dull beneath the sun. Shocksilver and Nightwing settled surefooted upon the largest exposed rock. Hawkwind sloped down towards the difficult landing site. A new fear grew within the fledgling. He was uncertain of the safety of this perch so close to the swamping waves. Hawkwind touched down, feather-soft, on the wrack. On his third pass the little one stiffened his wings so that he was gliding towards the adults. He approached too fast. His feet touched against slippery stone and he skidded and slid into Hawkwind. They both toppled at the edge of the rock and again were airborne. The old common tern squawked his annoyance and sloped away to land on a jagged reef close by. He turned his back to the arctics and preened his dishevelled feathers. On his second attempt the fledgling broke his forward motion so that he dropped the last few inches to land between his parents, almost as softly as they had done, though without the grace and dignity of their age.

Life, now, meant flight, the thrill of tense muscles, a blast of turbulence: the entire giant volume of the sky.

The adults hunted and brought their victims for the fledgling to satisfy his galloping appetite. He flew with them and watched them hawking across the shallow waters, their bills pointed down, their eyes discerning shapes where he could barely see movement. One by one, or together, they dropped upon the fish shoals, slashing away the lives of sand-eel, mackerel or elver in a cascade of silver spray.

By dusk the terns had reached the sands of the Naver estuary. Here, in the dunes, with the sound of waves a mere distant murmur, they nested through the quiet hours. At first, while a glow held in the sky they dozed with heads raised, as if still half alert; but later, when wind and tide were still, and the blades of marram grass stood out like motionless black needles in the northern night, and the forms of the dunes became obscure, they turned their bills into the warmth of their shoulders and slept: four touching shapes hidden amongst darkness and shore grass.

SEVEN

In the early morning, against the skirt of the sunrise, the flight lessons were continued. A hundred feet above the sea the terns banked, stiff-winged, and then as one body they dropped and hurtled towards the beach. The two adult arctics and Hawkwind, all larger and paler than the central beating figure, again rose, spiralling upward and levelling a thousand feet above the sea. Then the small one, confused and angered by the superior aerobatic abilities of the adults, thrust for height and curved up in pursuit.

For the rest of the day they flew, the fledgling struggling to match his parents' flight as, effortlessly, they surged off, and left him alone above the hostile sea. From half a mile upwind they called him, coaxing him towards them, their voices baiting him to thrust harder. They forced him in perpetual flight, whipping with their voices until he accelerated, until each beat was an agony, a wreath of flames about his chest. Shocksilver and Nightwing had a shared purpose; to drive stamina into their fledgling, to prepare him for his migration, his exhausting journey; to deliver him hence to the Atlantic Passage.

Soon the terns had crossed the North Minch and had

come beneath the shelter of Tolsta Head on the eastern slopes of Lewis. The sea was calm here and was green with plankton. Less than a mile from shore a shoal of basking sharks had surfaced and were heading slowly out to sea. They were over fifty strong, led by two giant females who weighed between them more then eight tons. A hundred triangular fins, up to four feet tall, waved above the calm shallows as the vast plankton-harvesting shoal swept out towards the deep water. The fledgling could see the cave-like mouths, six feet across and dirty white against the thick green depths, and then the rippling mountains of grey-brown flesh, each pushing up a V-shaped ridge in the calm water. Sharks brushed beneath with scarcely a sound, sleek silent power, awash in the Hebridean evening.

Half a mile behind the basking sharks a shoal of mackerel had also surfaced, taking advantage of the plankton bloom. Flickering bars of turquoise light betrayed their presence against the deepening colour of the sea. The terns caught the brief glint of life. In less than a minute they were above the spot, hovering with heads turned down, waiting for the right moment to dive.

Six fish moved apart from the shoal. Unaware of the watchers in the sky they nudged into the surface film. Hawkwind turned over, his shoulders pulled against his body. The arctics followed close behind. The fledgling watched them enter the sea: thwack, thwack, thwack. There was a flash as the whole shoal of mackerel turned down into the deep. The adults reappeared, struggling with the weight of their victims. Hawkwind had missed; but anyway he was not hungry. Shocksilver had stabbed a mackerel through the gills and it lay still as he lifted himself into the air. Nightwing had caught a small fish about its skull so that it kicked from side to side, throwing her off balance, as it fought. The fledgling dropped down until he was inches above his mother. He nipped at the fish's tail while the female remained motionless, holding fast on the mackerel's head. For a moment both terns were gripping the writhing body of the fish, Nightwing sitting on the sea, controlling the situation, and the young one beating at the air, maintaining his position as he bit into the fish's tail. Nightwing loosened her hold, passing the burden to her fledgling. He lurched forward under the sudden increase in weight and then began to climb, slowly and with great effort, away from the female. Shocksilver and Hawkwind were above, watching and waiting.

In a last bid for freedom the fish kicked and broke free from the tern's weak hold. It spun over, a flash of living gold in the evening light. Broadside it hit the sea and began to skitter along the surface, unable with its wounds to turn down to safety. The fledgling's hunter brain was alight, his stare fixed upon the flickering shape beneath. All apprehension about entering the sea left him. He weaved above the space where the fish was twisting away its life. For the moment nothing else existed in the bird's mind; just the mackerel's flank turning against the sun. Wings closed, he plunged down; a blur in the gathering dusk. Thwack, and he was gone beneath the foam. For seconds he did not reappear. Bubbles rose to the surface, marking his passage, and then these too disappeared. Nightwing grew anxious and flew above, calling for the young one. Then his body breached the sea, his wings slapping upon the swell as he pushed himself and his prize along the surface. Five paired marks of foam hissed in his wake, and then he broke free with his prize. He hauled far up into the sky where his parents' bellies and wings glowed a deep red against the dusk.

The four birds ascended into the sunset, watching the world tilt away beneath them, fading into the night. A cold rush of air stroked beneath their feathers. Soon the Aurora would flash in the northern sky and shortening days would push the migrants south. Meanwhile the fledgling, the hunter, above the adults, soared exultantly across the evening, reluctant to fall down into the folds of darkness.

EIGHT

The ice-cap thaw had slowed. Dwellers of the high-latitude summer, geese and terns, whales and fish, gradually moved southwards before the danger of the autumn dusk could take hold. The arctics and their old companion remained in the Hebrides. They were aware of an increasing activity as dense flocks slowly thronged above the white-sand beaches of the isles, as starlings collected in yellowing fields, as swallows and martins swooped with urgent energy for the evening hatches of sedge and chironomid flies above the lochs. Yet Shock-silver was not ready to turn south. The cold island waters were still packed with shoals of fish-fry. The borealis had not slanted its steel-blue signals of a dying season; the star-map suggested migration but did not demand it. The fledgling still possessed the mottled brown and buff coloration of extreme youth, though his underside was paler. In three months he had grown almost as long as the adults. His feathers were still dull, not quite ready for the high-speed journey.

Irridescent sparks of fish fled beneath them and merged into the twilight depths. The terns dived, Hawkwind slapping down clumsily but with speed enough to catch a fish. With migration only weeks, perhaps days, away his heart was on his kill. He no longer shared with the fledgling. His hunger was selfish and continuous.

When they left the shoal they rose, heavy and slow-winged, energy packed within them but not yet ready for release. Now the mainland grew out of the sea before them. The heights of Fashven and the mountains of north-western Sutherland drew nearer. The fading flowers of heather showed above the shore's white line.

The growling confrontation of rock and waves filled the air and often a quicker, sharper note crossed the tide. Whenever the adults heard this sound their flight checked or veered, and to the fledgling they seemed curiously alert, ill at ease with this alien note from the shore. Then the noise-shocks ended and the sea-sounds were master. The terns relaxed and crossed the battered cliffs.

Two men walked the silent moorland. They were a product of leisure-orientated Britain, hunters with money-bought freedom to roam the wilderness regions of northern Scotland. Often they had shot the ptarmigan and hazel grouse of the northern Alps. Together they had spent weeks in pursuit of the pheasants of the Ardennes, or in the meadows of Hampshire where the half-tame partridges were expensive but guaranteed; but above all they revelled in this new place they had found at the Atlantic's edge. For a price they laughed about they were given freedom to shoot rabbits and grouse over an area larger than they could have found anywhere else in Europe excepting the forests of Scandinavia and the rocky foothills of the Alpine Range.

One man carried a twenty-bore shotgun purchased for over £3,000 from a gun-smith in Soho, London. The

44

other held the blue-grey form of a small-bore rifle. The patterned metal and shining dark stock glinted with sinister suggestion. Both men were dressed in tweeds and carried small packs on their backs and bags around their waists for any game they cared to take. Already the bags were bulging with their success. Having walked many miles across the moor, the men were red-faced with exertion. Now, as they neared the sound of waves, they continued shooting but left their victims where they fell. Remembered numbers, and the carcasses they carried were good enough to demonstrate their skill back at the hotel.

In their wake, littered amongst the heather, were other marks of the gun-men's skill. Not half a mile from where they had left their car a harrier hawk lay upside down, loose-necked, in a gorse bush. Only slightly wary of the two men the harrier had winged briskly across their path two hours before noon on her way back to her nest. Simultaneously she had heard the shot-gun's blast and felt a fierce sting as her tail feathers were shredded. Then, even as she staggered, the gun's second barrel coughed its load and blew her out of the sky. Her fledglings, two miles distant across the moor, would wait many days watching the quiet highland sky for any shape that might be their mother.

Eleven grouse and a dozen rabbits had fallen by noon, some fluttering or kicking away their last moments head down in the wet peat soil. A merlin falcon had his left talon blown away, but he had escaped the second wild shot at his fleeing shape. Within a week either hunger or a blood-poisoning infection would kill him. Either way it would be slow at the end, and meanwhile he limped and stumbled over the bare rocks high out of sight and reach of a possible mercy shot from the hunters.

None saw the merlin fall, save the hunters' uncaring eyes, though many heard the shots. For an hour, while the men moved nearer the sea, not a single bird flew within sight. Rabbits crouched deep in their warrens, trembling in the silence, terrified that they might again hear the noise of men. A stoat sniffed uncertainly at the air. He stood on his hind legs and peered above the heather, his whiskers quivering, his eyes shining and alert. He moved out on to an open patch of sheep-trodden grass towards the carcass of a rabbit that had attracted him from a mile downwind. Three feet away from the carcass the stoat stopped and cringed backwards, frightened by the sudden smell of cordite. He lolloped back towards the heather and sat down, uncertain and wary. That smell was rare upon the moor, and when it came it meant danger. During the night, if clouds covered the moon, and if a fox or wild cat did not beat him to it, the stoat would approach the rabbit; but the risk was too great in the open light of day.

The fledgling hung beneath his parents, watching the crisp autumn light playing along the silver-laced edge of their bodies, the shimmering feathers, the sun-shot forks of their tails. With Hawkwind lagging fifty feet behind, the arctic terns cleared the cliff's summit and moved steeply into the sky. As if their energy was suddenly spent they canted their wings and together turned down towards the struggling shape of the old common tern. Their swoop broke into a smooth level flight three yards above the surface of the moor. A moth fluttered, velvet-bronze-winged, above the heather. Nightwing slowed and veered, her body hissing through the still evening air, her belly turned sunward in her last moments of sensuous

46

joy as she closed with the moth. She did not hear the gun-shot that obliterated the sounds of her dive, nor did she see the blast of lead that destroyed her sight. But she was not instantly felled from the sky. She felt a hot thud in her chest and pricks of fire across her head. She somersaulted, wings flaying at the air. Shocksilver and the little one were with her, calling, shielding her falling body with their wings. In those few seconds it seemed she knew they were there, for her wings stretched and her fall slowed. She thrust, briefly gaining purchase on the air; she climbed, turning until she was vertical, riding up on the evening currents. Her head and her chest were blood-streaked. It dripped from the streamers of her tail. Then she could fight no more and the pain faded to nothing. Her wings loosened and she tumbled to earth: Nightwing the global wanderer, with sixteen migrations behind her, was dead.

The men had spent the last of their ammunition. 'Did you see that?' cried the bearer of the shot-gun. 'Got him framed against the sunset! My last shot!'

'Tern that was,' replied the other. 'Never shot one of those.'

The men were laughing: today would make a fine story back at the hotel. They were still chuckling when three shapes exploded from the heather before them, freezing their laughter into gasps of shock. The terns aimed at the red faces, the wide eyes, the gaping mouths. The men waved their guns in the air in futile defence. They retreated, began to run, stumbled, swore. A wing slashed a two-inch cut in the cheek of the man who carried the shot-gun. He stopped waving his weapon and ran faster, flinching as another screeching white blur whipped past his face.

47

For half a mile the two men were chased across the moor. Then, as abruptly as they had begun, the frenzied killer-cries had gone and the terns had merged with the evening.

'Must have been dozens of them,' panted one.

'Those terns are wicked,' gasped the other, blood welling through fingers held tight to his face. They watched the sky where the birds had disappeared. They shook their heads and muttered obscenities: two small men alone on the silent, wounded heather-land.

The wind was a solid savage roar in his ears. His tail rippled and trembled with the speed of his travel. The fledgling pressed continuous power into his wings, throwing himself into a steep upward curve, firing away from the earth. The sea was beneath him now, and the shaking curve of the horizon, still lit into a narrow thread of gold. Shocksilver and Hawkwind rode with him; ten thousand feet into the sky's cold vault. Hawkwind lagged, the old dizzy feeling slowing him down; the pain in his neck. The fledgling stopped beating and started to turn, his momentum continuing to throw him upwards at nearly fifty feet per second. A foot apart, belly to belly, he and Shocksilver slowed their climb; tiny white specks joined by anger and shared loss. Their wings drew in until only the twinned swords of their primaries cut the air. Their tails turned starward, the dull silver wall of the Atlantic rushed up to meet them. At five thousand feet they flung out their shoulders and parachuted to earth.

They settled with Nightwing between them. For the first time since the shot there was no sound. They remained close by her body in the last moments of dusk, a mound of white clutching warmth; and when the light of

48

the moon became more intense than the western sky the female's body could barely be seen beneath Shocksilver's spread wings.

Later, the voice of the old common tern called from the darkness. The two arctics ascended to spend the night above the place where Nightwing lay. They flew again to great altitude, where a storm was beginning to shake the thin air. The invisible grip of turbulence pushed against their wings, but they held their position, wheeling six thousand feet above the moor and cliffs until dawn marked their wings with dull grey. Clouds drove together with a crackle of distant thunder and a mounting wind ran from the sea.

Through rain Shocksilver and the fledgling again fell earthward. Only a few feathers caught in sprigs of heather now remained of Nightwing's body. Neither male searched for her; the silent moorland hid the events of the night, and it did not matter whether a fox or a stoat had found her in the end. The feathers broke free to dance downwind and out of sight. One remained until it too was plucked away on a gust. Shocksilver stooped from his hover to intercept this last feather. Catching it cleanly at his first attempt he held it crosswise in his bill, so that as he flew it brushed and tickled at his cheeks. When at last he let it fall he and the fledgling were two miles off shore. Almost instantly the feather was swallowed by spray. For moments the terns hovered, oblivious to the storm. Then, gradually, they stroked away in the direction of the grey-black expanse that had closed off the southern sky.

NINE

A long creek of sand cuts almost due south into the heart
of moorland beneath the heights of Ben Loyal and Ben
Hope. A short, acid river drains into the southernmost
end, while two machair islands, called The Rabbit Isles,
block the two-mile-wide entrance to the north. The tide
runs in a confusion of currents past these islands, and
floods into the sandy basin. At the ebb long bars and
mounds lie exposed to the wading birds and seals for
which the creek is home. Silver birch and ash stand upon
the eastern slopes, heather crowns the west. Amongst the
birch, mid-way between the river and the islands, nestles
the village of Brae Tongue. Scattered farms spread towards the open moor and appear as sparse oases of
civilisation in the semi-tundra at the ocean's edge.

This is an ancient place which has retained the marks
and character of centuries gone by. The Romans never
succeeded in coming this far, but the Vikings brought
their crude and warlike ways. A broken fortress still
stands above and apart from the village, a constant
reminder of Scandinavian terror. Now there is a tiny post
office and a shop, and in summer there is a small influx of
tourists, for this is a restful haven amongst the wilderness

of the northern Highlands. The creek is known as the Kyle of Tongue, though to many it is the Kyle of Seals. For man and wild beast it is a sanctuary in hostile times.

Heavy rain and wind scoured through the ash woods. The late-afternoon sun shone cold beneath banks of heaped cloud. A glare, reflected from the windows of a car in the village, winked across the wastes and disappeared as a squall whipped off the sea. From the folds of racing cloud the terns materialised, their bodies irridescent as the brief snatch of sunlight reflected from the water which streamed across their feathers. They flew low to a sand bar close to the western shore. A herd of seals were hauling themselves up on to the bar as rain slashed patterns across the Kyle. For seals bad weather was merely a discomfort, poor visibility in the sea or a brief sting of hail in their eyes. For birds it meant danger; urgent need to find shelter while the wind turned against them.

Shocksilver led his companions to the end of the bar where they settled in a shallow sand-well. A piece of dead wrack formed a screen at one end of their resting place while the warm bodies of seals closed off the other.

The place chosen by the terns belonged to the herd leader. Oblivious to their presence she now came lumbering out of the sea, grumbling as she climbed the sand. When she was only three feet away the seal noticed the birds, the wary dark eyes staring back at her. A slow growl built in her throat and she drew herself up until her neck and chest were poised to fall upon the motionless terns, to crush them like so much seaweed. The growling stopped, the menace and aggression seemed cast away on the howling wind. For a moment longer the seal was hesitant. Then, gingerly and slowly, she leant forward, sniffing at the birds as if not trusting her poor aerial vision. Without sudden movement Hawkwind reached towards the massive bulk of the seal's head. When her whiskers brushed against his face he nibbled at her nose while the noise of sniffing and grunting filled his ears.

The storm drifted by, lit in sudden radiance, a living flash of white, then deep and dark, glowing crimson where it was edged by the last moments of dusk. The cow seal was asleep now, twitching her whiskers as the last of the rain trickled across her face. The fledgling and Hawkwind also slept, though Shocksilver was restless. Glimpses of stars through sinews of scattered cloud made him wary, for combined, they formed a map which was not aligned with the one in his memory. The need for migration was imminent; he could delay it no longer. He looked north, knowing what he would see there; the Aurora's relentless flicker, the ultimate migration signal. He turned back towards the seal's comforting shape which lay curled about the sand-well, shielding his companions and himself from the sea-draughts. He could hear her slow breathing, her stirring on the sand, and that too was comforting, like Nightwing's close presence and her quiet 'kik, kik, kik'.

The fledgling was woken by shrill calls of oystercatchers. He saw that Shocksilver was already awake, preening his shining flight feathers. The cow seal was still curled around them. Her fore-flippers moved as she felt the fledgling's bill nipping at her sleek coat. She turned to face him, her watery eyes clouded with sleep or non-recognition, or both. She felt his bill question through her fur, tugging at folds in her flesh. Eventually she leant

52

towards the bird and he heard the snuffling noise he wanted to hear. He smelt her heavy breath and he felt calm, reassured by his contact with this big warm beast.

Fresh cloud was building in the north. Petrels and shearwaters, only seen near land at breeding time or when bad weather drives them in from the open ocean, were seeking shelter along the coast. A storm petrel, a mere dash of dark feathers and wave-skipping feet, fluttered across the Kyle.

The flight urge was intense. The fledgling leaned his wings against the air and felt its strength, and the power of his muscles, taut like springs and ready for their nexus with the winds of the fierce Atlantic. He leapt from the sand, spreading his tail, a wide white fork catching the breeze. Then his streamers came together, his wings whipped to a blur, and he could barely be seen dashing across the bucking sea.

A shoal of fish fry sent puffs of sand flowering among the ripple patterns at the tide's edge. The fledgling adjusted his position with tiny wing movements and plunged upon the unsuspecting shoal. A big sea-trout, which also had been hunting the fry, leapt as the tern hit the water. His great muscular girth hung as he stood on his tail. The fledgling came up close to the leaping fish; two silver hunters transcending in a shared instant the boundaries of their own elements. Migration for the sea-trout was approaching its annual climax. In another month he would be on the breeding redds with the hen-fish. For the fledgling the inevitable journey, his first and most dangerous migration, was about to begin.

The terns climbed up above the moor. Nothing moved about them as they sped south-west, and yet the adults were aware that the sky was not as empty as it seemed; for here they were on the killing ground of the falcons. The smells and sounds of the coast were replaced with others which could not be trusted.

They rose towards Ben Hope where a buzzard wheeled above the rocky heights. A grouse's head stretched briefly above the heather. Quickly the terns moved on while Shocksilver searched for the danger he sensed.

The grouse's head flinched. Far above the buzzard two specks crossed the face of the sun. Their shadows, less than a smudge on the heather, smeared across the slope. The peregrine falcons were betrayed. Away from the glare their shapes became distinct; stiff-winged menace, soaring, waiting for the moment of the stoop. Shocksilver judged their height and distance in an instant. He spoke to the fledgling and Hawkwind in the danger tones of their kind as he hurried ahead, leading them towards a sanctuary which his own parents had shown him long ago, in other times of need.

The terns were now two thousand feet above sea level, and the summit of the mountain stood taller by another thousand feet. They swung around lichen-covered walls of rock and swept along the western face. Birch woods lay beneath them, and beyond stretched the inviting waters of Loch Hope.

Then the falcons dropped, talons held in to their bellies ready to be punched out at their prey. They became anchor shaped, one behind the other, accelerating along the chosen line of attack. At the moment of the pass, when they pulled out of their dive, they would be travelling at close to two hundred miles per hour. The terns sped close to the rock, the shelter of trees and loch still a long way below. A mountain uplift of air slowed their descent into the valley. 'Kee, che, che, che', cried Shock-

54

silver, abruptly levelling, his head turned towards the attackers. Instinctively Hawkwind and the fledgling turned beneath him. In that moment the falcons whipped past, air hissing across their powerful wings as they thrust out rapidly to slow the stoop. Bunched talons sprang and punched against empty air.

The fledgling could see the trees rushing up at him as a wall of green. Shocksilver was a few feet ahead, hurtling, it seemed, towards an impossible sweep of jagged branches. Then, the twigs plucking at their wing-tips, they were through the woodland canopy and manouvring along a tunnel of leaves and ferns. 'Gyake', the peregrines' hunting calls sounded through the woods. A young linnet, flushed out by the sound it feared above all others, ascended six beats clear of the trees before its neck was shattered by a falcon's kick.

The tunnel opened at the edge of a small clearing where a burn gushed across a short fall before sliding away in a silken run to the loch. Upon a bank of moss Hawkwind and the arctics set down. The sky showed beyond wavering leaves of birch, and occasionally a falcon brushed low to the trees.

Deep in the shadows of the wood only the slow movement of pearl-grey chests revealed the terns upon their perch of moss and stone. A sedge-fly fluttered before Shocksilver's face. He allowed it to pass for he had the desire neither to feed nor to strike. He was perturbed by many things. The falcons had hardly concerned him, except for the fledgling's safety; but the song of the sea-birds was nowhere to be heard. He desired the power of an ocean wind beneath his wings rather than a damp draught laden with the fragrance of pine and flowering heather, but he could not leave until the falcons had gone.

55

All these things, however, would have been nothing if the female had been with him.

When night came the three birds did not sleep. The fledgling watched the travel of a crescent moon through the trees. He too might have remembered how it had been with Nightwing on the nest, for repeatedly a sound came from deep within his throat, 'kik, kik'; and he nibbled at the ferns in the way she had cleaned his down. Surrounded by the alien creakings and rustlings of the woodland, and the loch's tideless waters, the terns anxiously awaited the first glimmer of daybreak above Ben Hope.

In a pale September dawn on an open Scottish shore the waves rolled, lapping upon the shingle, gurgling as they fell back in a seethe of bubbling laughter. A hundred pairs of eyes were awake and watchful as three terns quartered the beach, heads pointed down, thirty feet above the surf. Curlews and sandpipers trod together in the sandy shallows of a river mouth. Now and then they lurched forwards and their bills fidgeted beneath the surface. When again they looked towards the mark of surf the terns had gone: somewhere on the ocean wind, somewhere on their marathon flight.

TEN

She was four hundred yards long with a laden weight of four hundred thousand tons. She was the pride of the company that owned her, for her cargo was one of the most precious that any ship could carry, and she could hold more than most. She was an oil tanker of the Ultra Large Crude Carrier class, and her name was *Firedragon*. Each of her two propellers was heavier and longer than a London bus, and they were turned by engines as powerful as those of a battle cruiser. She represented the climax in the evolutionary design of the great super-tankers. Her kind was unlikely to be surpassed.

And yet the *Firedragon* was young, still brandishing her first immaculate paintwork of black and red, and still plagued by the teething troubles of any complicated and vast machine. But these problems were more of a worry for *Firedragon*'s insurers than for her owners. In the repair dock she was no more than an expensive encumbrance. On the high seas, heading home from Africa and the Gulf of Arabia, she was worth millions: and her faults were all minor.

Alone on the Atlantic the great tanker had weathered almost continuous storms. Colossal waves had passed along her entire length, obscuring all but the heights of the bridge and superstructure. All that earth's fiercest ocean could throw at *Firedragon* seemed to do little more than slow her down. Now, with the Lizard of Cornwall on her port horizon, she was two days out from the Thames estuary and the awaiting refineries. After having escaped a South Atlantic hurricane, *Firedragon* had been pounded by autumn gales north of the equator until she closed upon the restless coast of Britain. Here her tired captain and crew began to relax from the stress of the open ocean and prepare themselves for landfall. Here, off the wild shores of south-west England, on the autumn migration lanes, they grew careless.

The battle against the autumn weather had forced *Firedragon*'s crew of forty to remain below decks for more than two weeks. Much of the ship's fine-structure had been damaged — wires lay broken, aerials had been torn away and many pipes were bent and dented. As soon as the weather cleared, and *Firedragon* came beneath the shelter of the Cornish mainland, the work-teams started to repair the mess. Within a few hours, as if she had never thrust herself through a single storm, the tanker looked as magnificent as the day she left the ship-yard. No one noticed the leaking pipe beneath a steel weather-canopy far towards the bows. Neither did anyone notice the slight smell of petroleum vapour that collected there. The valves were not sensitive enough to offer warning of such a minor leak, and if the canopy had not trapped the pocket of vapour there would have been little danger.

On board an oil-tanker there are very few places where a man may smoke. The rules are strict even though the flammable hydrocarbons lie deep in the holds beneath several layers of plate steel, safe from the glow of a cigarette. One man aboard the *Firedragon* sat hidden from view in the bows, three hundred yards from the bridge. He had finished his work for the day, and as he had done so often before, he waited for his companions to leave him and return to the mess deck before he lit up. Lost in his thoughts he watched the sea, and felt *Firedragon*'s slow heaving upon the swell, while his cigarette burnt down to a stub. He smiled as he watched a tern flying above the distant bulk of the Lizard which lifted above the hills of water to port. 'Not long now,' he thought, as he flicked the butt over the side. It had been a long voyage.

Caught on the wind the discarded cigarette glowed brightly and was carried beneath the canopy. The man never realised the mistake he had made, for even as he turned away the petrol flash flung his body over the side.

On the bridge they saw the burst of flames before they heard and felt the shock of the explosion. They watched the immense weather shield spinning into the sea in the wake of the dead crew man. The first mate triggered the fire-alarm and the terrifying sirens carried their dreaded note across the entire ship. On board an oil-tanker a fire is more feared than a hurricane or a surf-lashed reef.

Within a minute the great propellers were in full reverse in an attempt to cut the forward momentum of *Firedragon*. The black stream of smoke and the gushing flames began to drift seaward instead of down the length of the ship. Men dragging foam-hoses and extinguishers ran towards the blackened bows, racing against the few minutes' chance they might have to control the blaze.

A pipe was torn in half and hundreds of tons of flaming oil spat over the bows. The hull was ruptured and the black cargo gushed into the sea. None of the men managed to turn a hose on the flames before the second

59

explosion dipped *Firedragon*'s bows hard down into the waves, and sucked the oxygen out of the air far beyond the limits of the rising fireball. The bridge window, which was designed to withstand the sustained force of a hundred tons of breaking ocean, fragmented and killed every man upon the bridge with the following load of heat and glass. The only men still alive on the tanker were those who had been aft, behind steel at the moment of the explosion; and they did not have long.

Firedragon was finished. The young high-capacity ship that was the pride of the oil company was coughing her precious tonnage into the sea and sky. Parts of her frame were already glowing at red heat while the remainder of her crew ran and screamed and dived into the oil-smoothed sea; her engines had stopped, never to be restarted, and her great bulk wallowed, fire pouring from within her holds. A cigarette, a careless action and a cloud of petrol gas was all it took; those and the fossilised remains of forests which had lived millions of years ago.

The young arctic tern had been watching the sea beyond Shocksilver's steady wings. A steep swell had been thrown up by the confluence of open ocean with the shores of Cornwall. *Firedragon* had loomed out of the sea like a vast reef. The fledgling descended towards the white curl of foam beneath the vessel's prow as if he expected sand-eels or baby wrasse to be feeding beyond the surf mark.

A cigarette's brightening glow and the smell of tobacco and petrol mingled into warning. Shocksilver called his command note, 'kee', and swept upwards, turning towards land. The fledgling hesitated, his wings brushing mere feet from towering steel. The first explosion ruffled his feathers. He panicked at the sound and swerved clear, while the suction of *Firedragon*'s motion pressed at his body. As he climbed he saw spinning shapes and growing fingers of flame licking along the bows. Then the note of the sirens grew around him; deafening, enfolding as a skua's wings. He could see the adult birds, already specks against the land; but their alarm calls were drowned by the tanker's thundering motion. Rapidly he drew away, low to the sea, so that soon the *Firedragon* seemed far away — until the second explosion.

The noise of the detonation momentarily preceded the shock-wave which met the fledgling with a force as solid as the wall of water into which he was thrown. Had he not been so close to the sea he would have been killed by the blast of heat. Even so there was barely time to feel the heavy smack as he was forced down. In the moments that passed he was aware only of a stifling numbness and the darkness of the surrounding sea.

Firedragon lay almost motionless; four hundred yards of blazing steel. A belching black cloud half a mile tall moved north-east, towards Cornwall. Not yet organised by wind and tide, long arms of oil flared and grew in the water. A roaring of flames and explosions as the holds burst open rumbled across the sky. Eyes upon the coast looked seaward towards the black mark on the horizon. Many knew what was to come, tomorrow or the day after. A tide black with oil and carcasses, and the stench reaching miles inland, boats spraying detergent on a slick covering many square miles of sea; sand and rock turned the same shining brown. But most of all there would be death.

The fledgling's chest hurt. Quite suddenly he was

61

aware of the heat around him. He drew in his wings and attempted to bring himself to a squatting position. At first, his body heavy with water, he failed. The strength of his wings eventually lifted him, and padding wildly with his feet, he was upright, all the time breathing at the heat. Droplets of oil, some alight, pattered on the sea around him. Gradually his hearing was coming back. He heard a noise like breaking waves and then it was like a strong storm, rising and falling. There was fire before his eyes, and the panorama of the *Firedragon* carcass. He fell into a trough, and in that instant there was no fire and only a gentle roaring above: and the blueness of the sea with air he could breathe.

That evening *Firedragon* was still ablaze. Along the coast people watched the twin sunset. The powerful orange light of the sun gradually dimmed until it was dwarfed against *Firedragon*'s aura, intensifying with each moment of the dusk. Helicopters and rescue ships moved as close as they dared, but all they found were a few charred bodies, black with oil. A slick, already five miles across, had formed and was drifting landward beneath the shadow of a great black cloud. The acrid smell of oil hung over the coast where so little time ago there had been the tang of weed and fish, and the cool sea.

She was beautiful as she died: beautiful and terrible. She lasted through the night, while the world learnt of the loss, and by dawn her cargo was killing and maiming sea animals at a rate of thousands per hour.

In many ways it was fortunate that *Firedragon*'s oil was of a high grade, rich in petroleum, since much of it evaporated and burned quickly, reducing the eventual size of the slick, minimising the number she would kill. Even so, when the feeble light of morning became stronger than the slowly subsiding fires, the watchers could see the vast shining patch of smooth ocean closing with the yellow sands. And when the sun rose only half the sky could be seen, the rest being obscured by cloud as black as a raven's wing.

Wherever the slick travelled there were men to meet it. Before the oil reached the coast they hosed it with dilute detergents, breaking it up into a thousand smaller slicks, easier to handle. On the beaches they worked with tractors and shovels, burying tons beneath the sand where, over the years, it would slowly be degraded by bacteria. They took lorry-loads of the viscous fluid to tips and burnt it; and they worked in their thousands all through the day, and would continue until the job was finished, until the tide no longer ran black.

North-east along the coast from Penzance was the tiny fishing village of Tregale. Like every other sea-bound village lying in the northern sweep beyond the Lizard, Tregale was the *Firedragon*'s victim. None of the two dozen families who lived there set off for work on the morning after the tanker accident. Their livelihood depended on fish, and until the oil was cleared there could be no fishing.

One of the youngest villagers was a boy called James. When his mother told him he was not going to school that day, he was pleased. Anything that stopped school could not be all bad. That at least was how he had felt in the morning. Later, as he stood with the others on the quayside, he was speechless and shocked to see the beach and harbour he had known all his life disfigured in such a way, overnight.

Through the day they worked, all of them, the old and the young, whittling at the enormous task of repairing

63

the damage. Here, on this isolated part of the coast, the spray-boats would be a long time coming, and it would be many tides before they glimpsed any results from their labour. James worked as hard as he could, wielding the heavy shovel and carrying bucket-loads of oil to the growing heap. It was towards noon, at low tide, when he had walked far out over the unrecognisable beach, that he noticed the birds. Almost beneath his feet a gannet, looking like dark kelp blown to shore, flapped its wings, desperately trying to fly, to escape the oil and the shape of the approaching human. It fluttered ten yards out and then splashed down, spread-winged and exhausted, into the slick. James tried to reach the gannet, but oil and water were up to the tops of his waders. For five minutes he watched the struggling shape, until it became still and merged with the suffocating dark blanket. When his eyes knew what to look for James saw more of the shapes, bobbing in the slow ebb swell. Most were silent and loose-winged, already dead. A few padded furiously with their feet and beat their wings upon the sea, struggling to rid themselves of the choking black fluid. They coughed and spat and pecked at their matted feathers, swallowing all they could remove. When death came it was with the agony of petroleum and aromatic hydrocarbons burning like fire in their bodies.

As the boy watched, a guillemot abruptly broke free of the sea and for twenty wing-beats it seemed that it might make it, that somehow it would climb into the cool clean sky and escape. Then with its heart bursting with the strain, and the poison in its guts, it fell, still clawing at the air, still fighting.

James called out as the bird hit the sea, and had it not been for his father's restraining hand he would have run out into the waves to save the bird, somehow to pull it clear.

'It's too late for that one Jamie. There will be others that we can help.'

'Will there be many, Dad; many like him?' The guillemot was head-down now, swirling and kicking, drowning in the darkness. Long before it became still James's father had turned the boy around, trying to distract his son from the animal's ugly death.

'But Dad, will there be many?' cried the boy.

'No, I don't think so, not many.' It was perhaps better to lie, even though James was bound to learn the truth in the end. The boy had been hurt enough for now.

'Go home, Jamie, you've done a lot today.'

'No Dad, please let me stay. I want to help. I'm all right.'

It was later, on the afternoon tide, that James saw another small dark bundle struggling in a clear patch of water. As it moved nearer he was able to scoop it out with the shovel. He ran up the beach, clasping the bird to the warmth of his clothes. Within minutes he had reached Cliff Edge, an old cottage high above the village, which was his home.

'What can we do for him?' he pleaded with his mother.

'We could take him to the sanctuary,' she said, 'but they'll have so many from farther up the coast. I think we ought to look after him ourselves. He seems in such a bad state.'

For two hours they worked with detergent-soaked cloths, rubbing gently at the frail body, pulling away matts of oil. Water streamed from the bird's eyes as soap and tar stung and bit at the membranes. In an hour the wings and tail were a light brown colour, though the breast and belly were still matted and dark. The bird's beak opened and a black stream of fluid ran out over its tongue. Then it collapsed with the strain, while soft human hands caressed its form.

When they had finished the bird was a bedraggled yellow-brown ball, too weak to stand or raise its wings, in too much pain to open its eyes. More fluid dribbled from its beak, and this time it was tainted with a smear of blood.

'It's a tern', said James's mother, watching the bird. 'I don't think he will live. Put him in the old rabbit-hutch on a bed of clean hay, and we will see what he looks like in the morning.'

The boy obeyed his mother, but did not go back indoors until it was too dark to see into the hutch. His father returned and sat weary and sombre before the fire. The family spoke of the *Firedragon* and oil, and of the ruin of their coast. After a while James asked, 'Is the oil worth it, Dad? Do we really need it that much?'

Not knowing quite what to say, his father hesitated. 'It's incredible; but I suppose we must do', he replied at last, although he did not really believe it. And neither did James.

It was not until late that night that *Firedragon* finally gave up. Almost all the oil was either in the sea or burnt off, and the blown-out holds were now awash with enough sea-water to sink her. Bow first she settled and slipped slowly away. Her deep, swollen stern rose into the air revealing the massive, silent propellers. For a long time she hung there as if reluctant to die. Then with a roar she slid away while the sea spat and clawed at her, as though angry at what she had done.

Back at Cliff Edge James did not hear *Firedragon*'s last

66

moments, but if he had he would have been glad that she had gone. Indeed he wished that she had never existed and come to die on this coast.

The next morning James was up before anyone else. Still in his dressing-gown he ran outside into the garden. His heart was pounding as he peered through the wire mesh of the hutch door. Two bright, dark eyes stared back at him. The fledgling was cleaner than the evening before and he was dry, warm in the nest of hay. His eyes still streamed and his belly stung. He could not stand, but he held his head erect, in the nesting posture of his kind. On seeing James he suddenly opened his beak and hissed out a defence call, but the sound came as a hoarse gasping noise, unrecognisable as the war-cry of the terns. Then he fell silent with only enough energy to sit and watch the wide-eyed boy.

At breakfast James asked, 'Are you sure the bird's a tern, Mum? He looks more like a swallow; his tail's all long and forked.'

'That's how you can tell them apart from gulls,' said his father. 'That and their more slender build and faster flight.'

'But he does look like a swallow,' insisted James, 'and that's what I'm going to call him.'

For three weeks, while the villagers of Tregale worked at cleaning away the tar, James worked at repairing the damage that had been done to the fledgling. On the third day the tern accepted a sliver of mackerel and drank some water that had been left in a saucer. By the end of the first week his plumage was free from the stain of oil, and he ate a meal at both dawn and dusk. Chunks of plaice and sand-dab he accepted, gulping them down by flicking his neck back so that the fish fell into his gullet. Cod he rejected, spitting it towards the hand that had offered it.

The young tern never attacked the boy's hand. In the first week he was too weak to stab at the frightening shape which moved around, finally stroking at his breast. And by the time his strength was returning, in the second week, it was almost comforting to be caressed by the soft touch.

During the third week something seemed to be wrong. The fledgling's health deteriorated. He had been making good progress, eating his fish and preening his feathers. He had moved continuously about the confines of the hutch; but then, one morning, he was quiet and sullen, ignoring the strips of mackerel that James offered. The next day, when the boy brought another meal, the tern's head was tucked under wing and remained there, immobile, even when James called. By the end of the week the bird's eyes were dull, possessed of the same lifeless quality as those of a zoo-beast, restrained from the freedom of the wild.

James went to his father and told him the tern was not well. The man reached out for his son's hand and when he spoke it was with all the sympathy that he must have felt for the boy.

'Jamie, you remember that book you read about the sea-birds?' His son nodded. 'The piece about the terns said that they flew more miles in a year than any other bird. That they follow the sun from Pole to Pole. Well, your bird out there is a tern and he has been kept in the north far too long now. What do you think is wrong with him?'

James looked at his father. After a while he said, 'I think he just needs to be free, Dad.' His father placed his hand on the boy's shoulder. 'Yes, that's what I think too.'

Alone the next morning, before his parents were up, James stood in the garden at Cliff Edge. He watched the sea, the white-maned waves restless in the cool October wind. Now that the time had come he realised that he had made the decision long ago, perhaps as soon as they had cleaned the tern, when he had seen what a beautiful creature had been hidden by the shell of oil. But it was hard to let go of something you loved and cared for, difficult to release it from your heart.

When James turned towards the rabbit-hutch his eyes were misty and red, and when he opened the door, slipping the latch and putting his hand inside, feeling for the familiar touch of the tern's breast, his face creased and his lashes matted with tears. In his gentle grasp the warm bundle did not move, as if totally relaxed, trusting the sobbing boy.

'You're going now, little bird, and I'm sorry for what we did to you, with the oil and everything. I'm sorry for keeping you so long.' His hands slowly opened, and for a moment the fledgling sat in his palms, looking at him. 'Go on Sea-swallow, please fly.' Then the bird was standing and turning to face the sea. His head moved quickly from side to side while cool air filled his lungs. There were no walls around him or the smell of rabbit, and there before him was the sea, a mere burst of wings beyond the cliff. And then in the instant of realised freedom his aching joints opened and the tern was airborne, rising steeply into the sky. Soaring and beating on the wind he climbed higher, sweeping a long opening circle around Cliff Edge.

'You really do look like a swallow,' whispered James, the words coming between sobs; 'a beautiful white sea-swallow.'

Alone with his private grief, the boy strained to watch the fading pale speck against the clouds. In the last seconds that the tern was visible, James doubted what he saw, for distance was distorted by tears. It seemed to him that two specks were falling towards the first. Then, all together, the three flickers of silver-white had gone. The boy's hopes were somehow strengthened by that last picture he would always remember, for he told himself that his sea-swallow now had other friends. In this, at least, James's hopes were fulfilled; but he wished for other things too. More than anything he wanted to follow, to hurl himself into the sky, so that they could still be together, he and the tern. Certainly he did not wish to be in the garden, with the cold of falling winter and the open door of the rabbit-hutch, swinging in the breeze.

PART TWO

Migration

ONE

In arrowhead formation the terns rushed southwards with Shocksilver leading, his wings beating determinedly, inviting no pause or question from his companions, demanding only faith. Rapidly the mainland set low behind them. At their starboard wings Wolf Rock, the last of the land, rose and guided them for an hour before it too slowly slipped away. A shower of hail smacked at their wings, although it barely slowed or concerned them: it was nothing compared with the joy of being close together once again, with their shared purpose.

Here they were, delivered at last to the Atlantic Passage, the great killer; the greatest of all. By nightfall the terns had pulled a thousand feet up into clear sky. A rush of cold air from the north-west hurled them away from the sunset. The night-sky guided their way and shone purple-silver from their feathers; three crescent-shaped ghosts drifting above the foam-scars of the ocean, silent on the roaring wind.

Orion had risen and the adult terns knew that to be able to see the winter constellation meant danger; but Shocksilver had migrated late in other years, whenever Nightwing had hatched a late brood. Like all other members of

73

his race he was not disorientated by a shifted star-map. He had flown nearly three-quarters of a million miles back and forth across the Atlantic. His awareness of the interplay between sun-north and magnetic north could not have been more finely tuned. This inherited ability to navigate mingled with his experience: Orion did not frighten him, it served merely to alert him. He pressed energy through his shoulders and doubled his speed, observing that his companions did not fall behind. He did not call them. Later, in a week or a month, he would need his voice to whip them on, but now they had enough strength to follow unbidden. With each meal snatched from the ocean's surface the fledgling's stamina increased.

The following day a rugged coast, like Cornwall's, marked their eastern horizon. The sea was a white flickering necklace of movement along the shore. Earlier in the season they would have paused here, in Brittany, to feed and to preen their delicate flight-feathers before facing the tortuous crossing of the Bay of Biscay. But they were too late for that and the beaches, battered as they were by white tendrils of autumn tides, did not attract them.

On across the Bay they flew, night and day, sweeping gradually south-west, the comfort of land always out of sight. Then the highlands of Galicia rose ahead. Here at last they paused and fed on tiny frogs upon wet grassy slopes above the sea. In darkness they flew again, faster than before as warm air from the Gulf Stream swept them on.

An anticyclone robbed the sky of cloud. For a week, as the terns flew along the steep-beached coast of Portugal, there was no rain; no water streamed into their parted bills to quench their need. Abruptly the land was out of

74

sight again. Shocksilver had turned them east, away from the open ocean, as intense sunlight drained their strength. Sea-swallow beat his wings by habit; but for a long time he had been decelerating, trusting the unfailing shapes of Shocksilver and the old common tern ahead and above him. Through the morning they had lost several hundred feet of altitude and the dazzling waters were now only a thousand feet below. The leader's voice was a spur. Almost in reflex the young tern obeyed. His breast muscles tightened, his pinions worked, pressed; there was little power left, just a wish to climb with the stronger adults.

At last there came a breeze on which to soar. An inverted bowl of ocean slid beneath them. Boats and ships materialised as occasional glinting dots, barely moving on a sleeping tide. They curled their wings and glided on the high-altitude winds. An aircraft roared by half a mile to the west and below them. When it had gone the rush of air across their primaries seemed louder than before.

A brown line grew before them, rising like a whale-back. The terns were planing, though the young one was not steady. He could feel the sun at his neck. The coast tilted in his vision until he found the strength to correct his attitude. Shocksilver flew close in to his side, nudging into him to help him keep stable. Brown merged into green; a marshland stretching from the shores of a wide river. Sea-swallow's eyes did not see the river. His sight was blurred. He knew he was falling but his wings would not obey him. He flew through heat, and again he saw the *Firedragon*, ravaged by endless towering flames; but all now was silent, without the crumping and thudding of the great tanker's exploding holds.

75

A thorn bush scratched at his tail and then he was down, his wings sprawled on unyielding earth. His chest trembled, unable to be still after so long under stress. Again he felt the oil-stabs in his gullet. Noise came through to him; relentless screeching and whistling at his head. Minutes passed until he recognised the voice of Shocksilver with its now dreaded note of command. Then it faded and became the only sound he wanted to hear, with its comfort and its strength; 'kik-kik, kik-kik'. He saw water drops clinging to his father's bill. He walked, following the older tern while using his aching wings for balance. Then he could no longer be certain of what he saw, for a twin sunset appeared before him. The suns were closing together and at the instant of their fusion it became clear that the lower of the two was a reflection. It ran like a dagger across the breadth of a river to end in a mass of wavelets each spangled with its own image of the dusk.

Water rushed through Sea-swallow's broken feathers and seeped across his hot flesh. It lapped about his eyes and head, and over his swollen tongue to douse his raging thirst. His wings were loose again, flaying the river surface into a sun-etched whirl of motion and sound. He sent out ripples with his shoulders and he felt their rolling spirit, their gentle energy dashing against his chest like a new pulse. The river held the substance of life, and its continuation.

The terns had reached the giant marsh south of Seville, a magnet for flocks of migrating waders and shore-birds. Agriculture was devouring the marsh, for oranges were considered by men more valuable than the curlew's sad music or the silver-bellied flight of the shelduck. Each year as winter falls in northern lands the birds return to this warm marsh. There are not many places left for them to go. Las Marismas, with the divided streams of the Guadalquivir river, is the last region of Atlantic Europe before the migrants must face the sand-fastnesses of North Africa.

TWO

A flight of wigeon passed like shadows through the early dawn of the marsh. A pair of greenshank sang to one another, 'tru-tru', as they trod on stilt feet through rotting grass stems at the river's edge. 'Whyt-a-whyt' cried a little sandpiper, annoyed by the greenshanks who poached places where he had chosen to feed on the marsh crustacea. A gentle breeze ruffled across a sprawl of lagoons where flocks of teal duck were making their winter home. The terns did not add their own voices to the rising tumult of bird song. Although they had been here a week they were outsiders, pausing only for the young one to build his strength before they set off once again. They rested upon a reed-fringed island where turnstones came to feed. Every afternoon these dumpy black and white birds came to explore the shallows of the island edge. 'Tuk-a-tuk' they grunted, as they flicked over small stones and weed stems in their search for caddis nymphs.

A pair of red kites slunk across the paleness of early morning. They headed towards the orange groves where they would compete with crows for road-way carrion left by the night's traffic. A shadow of silence spread as the marsh birds cowered beneath the kites' angled wings. When they had passed there was a new crescendo of song, and a brightening colour in the sky that filtered down into the reed shadows. The goshawks would come later, when the sun was higher, but meanwhile it was feeding time for the waders and duck, interrupted only by territory squabbles.

When the kites were no longer in sight the arctic terns and Hawkwind craned their heads skyward and turned to feel the early breeze fluffing out their feathers. They pointed into the draught and allowed their wings to sweep, to caress the air, until silently they rose above the shimmering light of the lagoon floor. They wheeled with slow powerful strokes before levelling, while the earth quickly disappeared into the morning haze below them.

Few of the waders noticed the dawn-flight. For a moment a godwit paused from driving her delicately upturned bill into the silt and watched the three white birds. Her last glimpse of them was of their flickering wings, rapidly fading against the enormous expanse of the southern sky.

The sun had risen above the Mediterranean and was shining black-orange along the Straits as the terns came away from land to feel the comfort of a following wind pushing them south. Already North Africa lay ahead; gateway to summer grounds.

The light was fast fading and sandhopper shrimp were skipping across the tide's edge, leaving a faint trail of phosphorescence in their wakes. The terns rode the breaker winds, before sweeping down as each wave combed across the beach. As it seethed back the sandhoppers leapt, dark against a brilliant background of foam. With perfect precision the birds caught the shrimp and ate them in flight, hanging, skimming, above the next advancing wave.

Porpoises were splashing in the shallow water close in to the beach as they tore through a shoal of sardines. Not far beyond the school a single mako shark cruised, waiting for a careless porpoise calf to move away from the protection of adults. A billion scales flashed in a scatter of gold. All was confusion and murder in the last moments of day.

Here on the narrow African flyway, the migration cross-roads of the eastern Atlantic, there were many hunters. Lanner falcons, smaller than northern peregrines, arrowed through skies concentrated with migrants. Horned vipers hid in sand burrows, waiting for a jerboa rat or a desert lark to come within striking range of their needle-sharp fangs. The western desert opened serebrown beyond hills which appeared to move in the wavering airs; and the noon-day sun pressed relentlessly upon tired wings. There was little relief at the ocean's edge with soft hot winds that were mere echoes of hurricanes a thousand miles out over the Atlantic. If a migrant paused too long here it would never find the energy to leave.

On down the great sands they flew, gradually turning with the coast, eastwards into the Gulf of Guinea. It was now a month past the equinox and the sun was approaching Capricorn. The air was humid above the coastal plains. For three days flight had been increasingly tiring in the thick, heavy air. Ahead of them were the mangrove swamps of the Niger delta. They had flown more than four thousand miles from the cold coasts of their home, and still they were not yet half way to their destination.

They thrust on through damp heat over calm, boat-crowded seas. Sea-swallow was frightened by men and their nets, frightened by shouts of fishermen, by the stillness and the dank smells of rain forest and swamp. Then trees gave way to open grasslands, the equator was crossed and the next distinct landmark would be the sands of the Kalahari on the Tropic of Capricorn.

The old common tern had almost reached his winter home. He could not travel as far as his arctic companions; his primaries were in shreds, his strength was sapped. He would have to remain off the southern tip of Africa from November through to March while he moulted and fed from dense fish shoals from the cold-water upwellings between the Namib desert and the Cape of Good Hope. In the spring equinox he would fly for the north and return to Scotland. There he would find his companions once again; if they had managed to survive their hazardous long migration.

Hawkwind faltered and swung away from the sea. The two arctic terns, the powerful leader and the young adolescent, began to swing with him towards the coastal Savannah. Then they circled and climbed. He heard their voices, 'keeray, kee, kee', though he could not climb with them. Silently he fell among the grass, thirsty, tired and dishevelled. It was enough to have reached this far, for the twenty-second time in his life.

THREE

The Southern Ocean threw its fury at the arctic terns. Feeding was impossible in the steep, breaking seas. Head-first, slightly aslant, they battled into the continuous west-to-east winds. Sea-swallow spent too much energy on the relentless turbulence until, watching Shocksilver gliding and skimming up ahead, he slowly found that he could do the same, that he could only join the screaming winds; they could never be mastered.

Ever onwards they travelled, south and east across the pathless wastes. They had entered the last leg of their hemi-global migration. They fought, then drifted with, the savage clockwise winds of the South Atlantic.

It was springtime and Antarctica had been released from immense cold. Sea-swallow was exhausted. The water beneath him was a lighter shade of blue than he had seen since they left Africa. Beds of kelp lay awash on the tide, wafting like drunken things with the sucking and pounding of waves. He and his parent had reached shallow water. They looked ahead into the twilight of the southern dawn and there, beyond the black and white smudge which was Drygalski Island, spread the great ice-floes. They had arrived. At only six months old Sea-swallow had flown more than ten thousand miles from his Scottish home. Following the sun, the urge within him and Shocksilver's guiding wings, he had completed his first outward migration.

There were huge flocks of birds here and it was more like home; gusting winds, fish-rich waters and cold. In the swelling light of December they fed, revitalising tired muscles, replenishing their slender bodies with a few grams of fat. Their internal clocks told them to feed and to wait through the brief southern summer.

Then, in the early days of January, their worn split feathers came away and floated off, merging with the ice-drifts. The silver-white adults, the grey-white adolescents, became drab and half naked. They stood or sat, incapable of flight, through the weak heat of high summer. But the food within them and the busy workings of their bodies sustained them as new feathers replaced the old. By the end of February they could fly again, and fed constantly in the perpetual daylight. The adolescents were now indistinguishable from the adults even though they were as yet incapable of breeding; but they were lean, swift-flying sparks, filling the sky above Drygalski Island with silvered wings and explosions of song.

It was March and the sun was falling from Capricorn into the increasing fires of Antarctic sunsets. It was time to turn again for the north as the blue-green Southern Aurora dashed the ice-plains with the colours of false daylight. The adults' attention was diverted away from feeding and moulting and waiting. Upon the bare icy rock-slopes, they looked for their flight companions and their partners. They collected into graceful silver flocks high in the red-and-orange dusk skies. Beating towards the north, this time flying into powerful westerlies, they fought their way towards Africa, the newly-lit memory of Europe and the Arctic spurring them on.

One of the last adults to leave was Shocksilver. He stood with Sea-swallow, quietly watching another swarm of terns sweeping across the sky. He spoke with his endlessly reassuring 'kik-kik, kik-kik', although it did not possess enough comfort for the young one. Shock-silver was about to leave. The adolescent, not yet ready to find a female and reproduce, had no purpose in the north. He would remain, alone, in the company of others too young to breed, in the southern seas, while Shocksilver and the great flocks returned to Scotland. One day, on the narrow African flyway, they would meet again and continue their shared adventure. Now the young tern was to be abandoned. He flew a short distance with his parent, feeling anew the exhilaration of migration. Shocksilver thrust rapidly forward and then, in the cold sky ahead of him, Sea-swallow saw his father's form dwindling into the distance. A call came downwind, 'kee-kee, keerah', and then it was snatched away by the howling wind. The young arctic tern was finally and completely on his own.

FOUR

Sea-swallow flew northwards, but he was confused, disorientated by strange stars, lost on the upwellings between Antarctica and Africa. Scotland was home, and the Isles, set in a lacework of foam; high mountains at the sea's edge, moorland and machair, and busy feeding with Shocksilver and Hawkwind; but now he was alone. He flew slowly, probing beyond the forty degree latitude in the middle of the Atlantic, calling occasionally to the empty wastes: one tiny fragment of life winging across the ocean's unfeeling tracts.

He was learning, continuously collecting information which one day would guide him. The map was in the sky; he set it into his mind. There was no comfort in the mighty waters beneath him as he followed the cold-water currents which led him north.

Through the months of southern winter the young arctic tern very slowly followed his memory. He hesitated in the spinning winds above South Africa before continuing as far north as the Kalahari sands on the Tropic of Capricorn. He probed on his false migration, he escaped the southern night by following the rich fish-shoals of the Benguela Current. Then, in September, subtle temperature and wind changes turned him about. His confusion had gone. Bravely he put the Tropics at his tail and searched the sky until he found powerful north-westerly winds.

He flew as if he were weightless, planing and banking as he gripped the air. He shrugged clear of a ridge to see savannah ahead sloping away to the ocean. 'Keeray', he called across the plain; but there was no reply. He accelerated until he was a pearl flash twenty feet above the grass and then fired out and away from the coast; a silver sea-bird having transcended the bounds of youth. Allowing spray to punch and crack against his shining feathers and run in jet streams from the prongs of his tail he curled away from the foam. Soon he was settling to the rigours of sustained flight. Panning ahead was a pale sky that was the dawn of a new southern summer, with its seduction of cold, clean air.

In the weeks that passed Sea-swallow was carried south and east from the Atlantic into the southern limits of the Indian Ocean. The winds were as he remembered them on his first migration to Antarctica the year before; but they were stronger, heavy with sleet and hail. He was early. No other arctic terns flew with him. A shearwater's slanting shape sometimes kept him company in the grey-blue expanse; or a petrel, a skipping dash of black, low in the water valleys, gone in seconds through a tunnel of spray. These were birds which had adapted to an existence above open ocean. Both were dependent on being able to remain in the air with the minimum of effort. The shearwater had long slender wings which were held stiff so that the bird could glide for hours without a single beat; but the petrel's body was no larger than a man's fist, with tiny, quickly working wings and, unlike the shearwater, it escaped the wind's force by dodging between the shifting barriers of waves.

Faced with the unceasing winds of the Roaring Forties Sea-swallow began to tire. Here, in early November, he was flying at the blizzard's edge, alone in southern twilight, and hungry. Relentlessly the air-flows carried him south; down, down into the cold.

In Antarctica the pack-ice was receding: the light did not fade. Blues and greens and golds competed in a furnace of colour which was colder than it appeared. Petrels and shearwaters, prions, penguins and Sea-swallow were drawn by the krill; hunting seals followed, and the great whales, casting their breaths, like flames, against the walls of icebergs.

The tern drew now upon his ancestral knowledge. Like the salmon, the baleen whales and all the birds which risk long journeys across the great oceans, the small bird was guided by a wisdom that had been passed down through countless generations, if only as a subconscious tool for navigation.

Onwards, struggling, he fought towards the twelve million square miles of ice and ocean bound by the Antarctic Convergence, the junction between cold southern waters and the tropics. Snows tore across his back.

Sea-swallow's tiredness had now become exhaustion. The wind was blowing at over a hundred miles per hour, rushing down from the glaciated heights of Greater Antarctica. It was snowing and visibility was down to a few feet as the blizzard tore horizontally out over the sea. The young tern beat directly into this white gale which howled around him. He could not have known that he was not even moving forwards, that relentlessly he was being forced back the way he had come. It was a last barrier, one which had sneaked in to rob him of victory when he had come so far. Neither could he have known that Drygalski Island was only ten miles ahead. If it had been ten feet in front of him he still would not have been able to reach it.

Abruptly the snow stopped but the wind blew even stronger than before. Sea-swallow faltered, stumbled, and fell to the waves. He had no strength left; he sat, a tiny trembling glint of white, and listened to the Antarctic's mocking spirit roaring beyond the crests.

FIVE

Greyback, a wandering albatross with a wing span of nearly twelve feet, was astride the savage plateau gale; but it was nothing to him. Having lived now for more than forty years he had circumnavigated the ice-shelves many times, and had come to know them better than any other bird. The southern fringes of all three great oceans were his home, and the constant drift of the Roaring Forties was his only master. Once he had known the joy of flying with a female; together they had nested and raised young upon the lonely islands at the edge of the Meteor Deep, until a fighter pilot, eager for target practice, had found her and shot her great body to fragments. Since that day Greyback had not kept the company of another of his species, and had patrolled the edge of the Antarctic blizzard: one with lonely freedom.

The old albatross had flown with Japanese and Australian whaling fleets, and alongside the baleen whales he had fished, surrounded by the slurping and bubbling of their feeding. He watched the passing of the giant mammals and shared their loss when man intruded into the summer thaw. He had desire to do little more than wander the pitching reaches of the Southern Ocean. Tire-

89

lessly he winged across his destiny, gliding hundreds of thousands of miles to pass the time. The memory of the years he had spent with the female's graceful shape was all he needed to shut out the emptiness. Sadness, and a half-remembered warmth flew with him.

Greyback could not have known that a young arctic tern, not a quarter his size, would bring something more to occupy his slow, pensive mind before this summer had gone.

The fractured ice along the shores of Drygalski Island passed beneath him. Few terns had yet arrived so he was not troubled by their raucous abuse. He glided across the ice-rim and came out over the sea which was snatched up and thrown by a million white fingers of the shelf gale. Among the foam marks he noticed a small feathery shape and as he passed overhead he saw it move. He eased his left wing down, coming about to face the wind, and began to descend. His head tilted from side to side and his big dark eyes watched. Then he called, a deep growl-like noise, 'grah'.

Sea-swallow heard the voice of the albatross. He looked up at the sky, beyond the towering waves; but his eyes were dull, only half alert. The airborne colossus glided serenely into view. Terrified, Sea-swallow spread his own wings and screamed his defence cries; 'che-che-che-che'. Then his head lolled, exhausted, even by this tiny effort. The steep swell lifted him and again he saw the majesty of the great bird closing rapidly from up-wind. He crouched so that only a spitting red gash of bill could be seen against a grey-white background. The air hummed as the albatross passed overhead.

Twice more, as Greyback flew by, Sea-swallow sent his abuse upon the air; crouching and angry, ready, even with his fatigue, to burst clear and drive his wings at the big bird's head. On the fourth pass Greyback called out again, 'grah', deep but without malice. There was no reply; only the huddled, wary heap of ruffled feathers. Instinctively now the tern realised that the albatross, though powerful, meant no harm.

On the fifth pass Greyback watched the slender bird push out his wings as if he wanted to climb back on to the wind. Then the wings folded and the tern fell back into the deep curve of the waves. Greyback had seen this many times: the tired early migrants setting down on the swift running sea, with only a desire for a few minutes rest, to turn head under wing and relinquish their spirit to the silence and the sleep of the troughs. After weeks out on the open Atlantic, with weather deteriorating all the way, they did not realise that they were so close; if only they could fly through the last wild blizzards. For the others who travelled with the sun it was easy, but for those who flew many thousand storm–filled miles, even the strong rarely forced themselves through the last barrier.

Greyback turned until he was gliding along the waves, at right angles to the wind. His six-foot wings curved a little until he rode the rushing draught along a crest. Then he watched. Two hundred feet ahead he found what he was looking for. He rolled off the draught and soared down the long buffeting slope. Now he had to move his wings, beating them slightly to maintain his stability. Then he was in the silence, two massive walls of green water rising each side of him. He slowed his speed to just above stall. This was dangerous for an albatross. He did not have the wide short wings of a kestrel, or the quick flickering breast muscle that could maintain him in a hover; but Greyback had taken risks on wild seas before; the ocean was not his enemy.

There in the silence, his wings and his eyes heavy, the arctic tern responded to the hypnotic influence of the slowly moving albatross. It appeared so easy to mimick Greyback's flight. Sea-swallow's webbed feet stroked down into the sea and his shoulders swept out. He was aloft once more, with the same trembling pain in his wings, the same struggle over an infinite expanse of water. And yet here in the wake of the giant it did not seem as bad as before. Greyback knew where to turn, knew how to change the wind from howling demon to ally.

He had spent almost a month with barely any sleep, always on the wing, struggling through storm and snow for hundreds of miles; and now here he was hanging beneath the albatross, allowing this huge animal to take him where he would. Held by the soft suction of Greyback's travel, shielded from the driving white of the southern sky, Sea-swallow moved his own body at the command of the Old One. Together they rode the south wind: together they outflew the shelf-gale.

A mauve-shot wall of ice hung above them, towering up into the pale Antarctic sky. The two birds sat together upon a long beach on the eastern slopes of a great iceberg. There was almost no sound. Like a plain of silk the sea spread away from them, broken here and there with slabs of ice, some vast but dwarfed by distance, others small and jagged, barely moving on the gently throbbing swell.

As soon as they had outridden the storm the wind had dropped to a whisper, and they had come to a sea awash with drift-ice. Sea-swallow flew slightly above and behind Greyback, lifted and guided by the eddying slip-stream of the big bird. Soon the albatross found a suitable landing site, and soared in from half a mile off to end with a flurry of beating wings and slipping webbed feet. An albatross is designed not so much for landing as for gliding, but Greyback understood that the tern needed to rest after such a long passage; and anyway, with the wind now more than forty miles distant, it was easier to wait upon the ice than to beat at still air.

For several hours, as the air warmed slightly with the sun's climb, the young bird dozed and trembled, his spirit dashed by the thousands of miles he had flown. To realise it was over, so suddenly, with muscles still burning at the memory, was difficult. Every moment he expected to be awoken by the screaming wind, to struggle once more against the Antarctic's savage claw. He had fought the swirling, buffeting currents of the Atlantic and had ridden the contours of the sea, the ever changing, ever mobile hills, where, alone, he had danced on the spray. Even the squalls of the tropics had not brought him down as they had done countless others. Instead he had risen a mile above their force and from the silence of the clear, cold blue he had watched their tempers rage; but his body, attuned as it was to the moods of twelve thousand miles of ocean, had not fulfilled its greatest purpose; and his mind, alert and aware of things that only his kind could know, was restless. It might have been possible to have come this far with only his own resolve and strength, and with what Shocksilver and Hawkwind had taught him on their shared migration; but it seemed that Greyback had come to take him through the last barrier, to protect him from the sky's power; for there had been days towards the end when the mesmerising wash of the

Southern Ocean had tempted him too low towards the snapping venom of the waves, and he had appeared to be flying deeper into a never-ending storm. The albatross had brought him to this silent place where he could sleep.

The Antarctic tide ran softly beyond the shelf. Towards evening, while the beach on which they sat lay in a deep orange shadow, the albatross moved nearer to his new companion. Perhaps he had been touched by the courage of the small, lonely bird. Very few migrants that he had found in the storms of years gone by had been brave enough to follow him; or it might have been merely that he remembered the years he had spent with the female and her chicks on the islands. When he awoke in the gloaming of the southern night his starboard wing was open, in the nesting manner of his species, enveloping the fragile shape of the sleeping tern. A soft purr of contentment stroked against the walls of the berg. After a winter searching for squid and krill through the short wild days farther north, Greyback the Wanderer had returned, this time not alone, to the edge of the Antarctic continent.

During the next month, while Sea-swallow recovered and built up reserves of strength, the two birds did not part. In that time they flew twelve hundred miles of coastline, from Drygalski Island to wind-raw Dalton Iceberg Tongue. Often they were far out of sight of land or ice, coming away from the open ocean only when high winds drove them south, or when shoals of krill extended on warm currents like rich veins pumping into the ice. They did not remain long on the ice pack, since the wind was not constant enough for the needs of Greyback's gliding flight; the old albatross did not enjoy *actually moving* his wings.

One flash of motion, high above the ice-scape, grew and became a distinct bird shape. A long time later a speck of silver could also be seen close by. The albatross and the tern together hesitated and dropped rapidly towards the jagged pinnacles of ice. They vanished for a brief moment and then, lifted by gusts from the north, they were clear, flapping up, white and grey into the empty Antarctic sky. The floes, woven with webs of blue, raced beneath them. Greyback's bill clattered and at his command the two birds curved away towards the open sea. Beating, side by side, they covered twenty miles in an hour, though it seemed an instant in the short time since they had met.

Greyback could not remember much about his first year: a time when he sat on or walked over the surface of a grassy island hill. He had been with his parents for three months of the twelve, waiting for them to return with food the next day, or the next week. The lapse between visits grew longer until, at the end, three weeks had passed since his last meal. It was then, as an ungainly mass of bones and feathers, with a wing span of seven feet, that Greyback had set himself free on the Antarctic wind. Then there had been a gulf of years during which he had learnt what, in his hostile environment, could be trusted and not lead to danger. In an ocean full of leopard seals and hunting whales, and a sky quick with the venom of violent storm, there had not been much to befriend him on his lonely wanderings.

The times with the female were not such a vague memory, although they were short, and twenty years had gone by since he had seen her body explode beneath a rain of cannon fire. And then there had been another gulf of seemingly timeless, lonely flight, at the blizzard's edge.

Three miles off the shelf the two birds passed over acres of calm water. Greyback's head jerked from side to side, while his wings lifted him along fifty feet above the opening panorama of ocean. Something pink shone from just beneath the surface. The shape undulated, growing and shrinking as it moved slowly along. Greyback's course veered until he was slowing to a stall, poised above his target. His wings closed and head-first he plunged down, sending water six feet into the air as he crashed into the sea.

Sea-swallow circled once, calling for his friend, watching the patch of bubbles which marred the otherwise empty sea. The albatross reappeared with the limp form of a foot-long squid held firmly in his bill. They feasted, the tern on the dismembered tentacles and Greyback on the body, and then, hunger satisfied, they floated on the shelf tide, riding the summer-soft swell and bumping together in the shallow troughs: two companions of the wing, linked by circumstance.

For another month the sun did not leave them, brightening their world with perpetual day. They slept in grottoes in the hearts of wilting icebergs, drops of water plinking into pools on the floor; or on the wing a mile up in red skies, soaring across the dusk-dawn of the Antarctic wastes. They glided for three hundred miles over the snow, wings tip to tip or drifting quietly apart, their bodies afire against the low sun. No bounds restrained them.

Out over the sea a right whale sent a twin spout on to the breeze. Ten miles distant Greyback saw the quick shock of white. His flight sloped and he began to descend, his companion following fifty yards behind. Another mark of vapour showed against the waves.

The whale closed her great mouth. A ton of cloudy water gushed across her baleen, and her tongue slopped noisily over a giant mouthful of sweet krill. She swallowed, and her black tail, ten feet across, drove her deeper into the plankton cloud. She had followed the sun across the South Atlantic from the shallow coast of Patagonia and the Falkland archipelago to find seas so rich in the food she needed. After another month of feeding she would swim again for the archipelago and the north, and spend another winter searching for the male her heart desired, though for five years now she had found only calves or females. The pall of the surface showed above her. She lifted her head and threw her breath into the sky. Again her mouth opened and her tail thrust her on.

High above, the two birds circled, watching the right whale on her harvest. A square mile of ocean was reddened with the concentration of the krill, and yet the whale looked huge, even against this background of heaped life. Her head, encrusted with calcium and barnacles, breached the sea, and a roar like a gun-shot filled the sky as she blew. Sea-swallow flinched, clawing his wings at the air to pick up speed. Greyback's bill clattered, calling him back: there was nothing to fear from the great whale.

The ships would come soon; either those brandishing harpoon cannons or those with nets and suction apparatus, hoovering the sea for krill. The right whale would be safe this year; for her kind was protected in a last bid to drag it back from the brink of extinction; but the plankton she ate was now the target of the ships, for men had learnt that more profit could be made from harvesting the fundamental levels of the food web than by searching for the relic species of the giant whales.

The arctic tern hit the sea. In every direction the shrimp-like bodies of krill flickered and merged into a pink-white cloud: stacked energy, fed by the sun and the upwelling of phosphates and silicates driven to the surface from the Antarctic deep. He could not miss. His bill closed and in a moment he was sitting upon the sea, gulping down his victims. He had not learnt, and never would, how to eat krill or fish while under water, as the penguins did on their mass attacks. Again he flipped over, and down into the sea.

Before him, ten feet away through the murky water, the right whale closed her great jaws, repeating the feeding sequence that she had performed so many times before. The bird was caught in her wash, spinning in the eddies of her travel. A huge flipper stroked beneath him and forced him to the surface. Without knowing how, he was sitting on the sea, watching the whale pass under him; the massive dark girth, so close, so gentle, slipped across the deep, and then her tail, blasting upwards, stopped a foot below him: poised power that could drive her across the southern ocean in a month. Entranced, Sea-swallow barely noticed Greyback swimming a few feet away, totally at ease in the close presence of the whale.

For a week they stayed with her, circling overhead, sitting in her wake or feeding with her. When she slept her back wallowed above the swell and the tern set down to sleep on her, or to peck at the barnacles on her thick hide. Then one dusk, in a flurry of swirling water, she set off beneath the ice.

If they had possessed her language the birds might have called their farewells, their wishes for good speed to the archipelago, their hopes that she would soon find the male she needed; and for her safety on the Southern Ocean. Instead the two companions sat on the turbulent water of her passage until they could no longer see her against the enormous ice scape, and the sound of her breath faded upon the rushing breeze. At least she was safe, deep in the summer floes.

Stationary, twenty feet down in the sea, a leopard seal waited a hundred yards out from the shelf. Small slabs of ice rolled and bumped in the ruffled waves, and the water was patched with shoals of krill. Adélie and emperor penguins flapped through the shallows, taking krill as they swam between the sanctuaries of ice-shelf and berg. The leopard seal was eleven feet long, and he could remain submerged for up to half an hour searching for his prey — squid, fish or bird — while his mate and her pups waited on the fast-ice. Quietly he inched his way out amongst the floes, listening to the voice of the Antarctic telling him where to swim, where to hide.

Krill tickled along the seal's belly as he waited, his ears alert to the sounds rustling about him. Far away he heard waves lapping against the walls of a berg, and the sea hummed with life. His flippers stroked him through the tide and a cloud of krill hung above him, shutting out the light. He hid there in the mid-deep, his hunter brain alert and ready.

Plop, plop, plop, a flock of adélie penguins flung themselves off the ice. Once in the water their clownish appearance on land was gone and they were streamlined creatures of the shallow seas, water acrobats finely tuned to the whims and variations of the cold shelf current. En masse the penguins swarmed through the krill, their bills shutting in a cacophony of snapping sound: the symphony of the hunt echoed about the drift ice.

Then another sound, not much louder but more sudden than the others, filled the sea. The seal had chosen his moment well, had held himself motionless in the gloom until the pale bellies of the penguins criss-crossed above him. His flippers fell flat against his body while his tail drove him into the attack. A thud stamped across the tide and then another, and the sound of the seal's jaws crashing and tearing: three penguins lay dead in his wake and another fell limp between his teeth. They would perhaps be enough for the morning, enough to help build a thick layer of blubber to protect him from the cold of Antarctica.

Closer in to the shelf Greyback and Sea-swallow plunged into the sea upon another collection of krill. Neither had seen the leopard seal's kill minutes earlier. The sea was again at rest, a cloud of penguin blood merging with the plankton. Greyback was back in the air first, for krill were poor fare for an albatross, and hardly worth the trouble of wetting his feathers and struggling in the calm air in order to become airborne. Usually he did not dive for them, but skimmed the surface and snatched them up with his bill. The arctic tern fed on, flipping himself over and down after resurfacing, returning each time with one or a pair of the crustacea in his bill. Greyback winged quietly over head, watching his companion feeding, happy to wait in the sky.

A shadow moved out from beneath a slab of ice. Sea-swallow was resting on the surface, his eyes flicking from side to side. He had not noticed the rapidly approaching seal. Greyback's wings moved into a hollow curve, slowing him instantly to a stall. Then, before he could have had time to think, he was diving, shoulders pushed forward, a growl mounting in his chest as he fell.

A yard from the seal's head Greyback crashed down, sending up a shower of spray and foam. It was enough to distract the seal's attention so that the tern could fire himself clear of the surface, before the jaws closed. Now Greyback himself became the seal's target. He had met these carnivores before, knew how fast they could turn, and how determined they were to catch their prey, knew that they could kill and skin their victims with a single movement. But never before had the circumstances been like this. He had always had a strong breeze to aid his escape, or enough distance between himself and the attacker. This time the seal was almost on top of him, and even if Greyback managed to reach the surface there was no wind to give support to his only means of escape.

Somehow he was there, beating his six-foot wings on the sea, trying to find the lift he needed. The surface foamed in his path and the dark shape of the leopard seal came out of the deep. He could hear the great wall of water building behind him, knew that if that washed over him it would pull him down, and the jaws would not be far behind. His belly came up; still his wings smacked against the water while his feet trod faster at the surface. He could sense the seal's great head almost at his tail. He needed only another moment − one wing missed the surface on the down-stroke − just another few seconds and he could be airborne again. A blur passed him by and a screech filled his ears, 'keerah'. Sea-swallow shot into the sea at his side, almost at the seal's neck, giving Grey-back the time he needed. Both wings were clear now, and the albatross drew his feet up and soared in a long beating turn above the ice, cutting back the way he had come, ready to dive again.

The tern was up, poised, two feet above the seal, his wings rapidly working the air. A bulge formed in the sea beneath him, and the seal lurched his head and shoulders at the insolent bird, roaring his anger, his huge dagger teeth exposed, yellow and chipped by many years of hunting. Steeply the two birds rose up into the sky, soaring away across the shelf, their narrow escape lending power to their wings.

With each passing day their friendship had grown stronger. It had been three months since Greyback had found the tern, and in all that time they had not been apart. They had flown half the circumference of the Antarctic Continent, pausing to feed, and to drink the melt water from icebergs, or to rest side by side upon the sea. They had shared each other's ways, learning, content just to be together. Half a summer had gone and yet it seemed that the storms of spring had only just ended, that only a few days earlier the young one had been fighting his way through southern blizzards and Greyback had been alone, a hermit of the Antarctic wind. They had been separated by half a world, the length of a great ocean, while migration and fate had drawn them to this same place, to share a summer, to give each other the knowledge of another race; and together to fight their enemies.

In another week they had come to the ragged coast of Victoria Land where vast mountain ranges towered two miles and more above the glaciers. Bare rock showed in patches where the ice could not grip. Cloud hung about the peaks and the wind hurled spumes of snow at the sky.

102

A distant sun lit the waste-land into a silver world of cold where little moved except fragmenting clouds upon the mountain gales.

Greyback turned with the coast so that they flew the seaward edge of the glaciers. Here the water was heavily littered with icebergs, and soon the two birds rose upon the early, broken reaches of the Ross ice shelf. For many days the weather held and they continued southwards, the line of the Transantarctic mountains rising to starboard. The ice thickened beneath them as the warmth of the ocean lost its strength and blizzards forced them up into more stable air-streams that flowed from the high ice plateau.

It was a colossal haul upon the mountain wind; but Greyback had chosen the time and the route well. It was now late February and the air was not yet cold enough to freeze their lungs. After the initial climb across Ross shelf, Greyback had found the air currents they needed, for he had flown these high wastes before. They flew along a shore where rock was split by tendrils of ice and then held suspended above the sea by the power of a glacier's grip, until the sun melted enough ice for the colossal slabs of stone to fall crashing into the sea.

The usual route of migrating flocks was to fly between the 70 and 60 degree latitude, but that way would take a month, whereas if Palmerland was calm and allowed them through, the journey would last only a week or two. The albatross knew that they had to reach the Atlantic soon, for Sea-swallow was drawn there by something much stronger than their friendship.

Across the last few miles they dropped a thousand feet. Ronne shelf lay deep red below them, awash here and there with dark patches of islands. Sea-swallow was tired; he had never flown over such terrain. His lungs were stinging with the cold, and his wings pressed hard at the thin air. They had been many days away from open water, and he longed to see a widening expanse of blue, instead of the endless ice; but now at least he could smell the salt not far off, and the wind was damp. Dusk fell across Antarctica, shining deceptively warm against the Touchdown Hills and the stacked rows of Neptune Range, darkening the colour of the opening ice desert of the shelf.

The flight urge drew the arctic tern. He had felt the new cold in the south wind at the ice rim, had seen the plains knit and fold together, and observed the wild grey moods of the sea. Emperor penguins collected into snow-draped flocks, like ice-still sentinels beneath the southern dusk. Sea-swallow knew that he no longer belonged here with the albatross. Greyback had taught him how to survive at the blizzard edge, had shown him what he must fear; that the greatest danger was to trust too much, and that Antarctica was a friend only if she was not insulted by carelessness. The albatross still flew with him, his bill chattering through the dusk; but the northern bird was unsettled. He would be flying around the face of an iceberg, stark white against a low sun, but what he saw was lichen-covered granite, encrusted and streaked with the lime of a great breeding flock. An avalanche of ice at a glacier's ocean foot became a waterfall, its golden colour not the sun's effect but peat stain from a moor that existed in Sea-swallow's mind, and an ocean's distance away. When the two birds rested, when the tern's eyes were closed and the babble of a penguin rookery crossed the ice-plains, and the sea ran hard along the shelf, it was

104

almost as if he were back at the cliff in Scotland, the warm purr close by not Greyback's contented sleep, but his parents' nustling at his wings, one each side. Greyback sensed that soon he must lose his friend. But together they had passed a fine summer.

The sun did not rise far above the ice and for long periods remained hidden behind thick cloud. A cold air-mass from deep within Antarctica overflowed the mountains and rushed, whining, across the plains.

At the end of their summer together the tern and the albatross stood on the edge of the shelf watching the hypnotic motion of the South Atlantic, and the broken fragments of ice, undulating and bumping on the tide. Soon the sun would not rise above the eastern sheets at all, and the silent drifts would lock and become one: nothing but the blizzard would move through the darkness. Both birds would have to be far away by then, although neither of them wished to part. Next year they would find Antarctica again: but not each other.

Sunlight slanted through dense cloud and cast a palette of warm colours across the floes. Greyback stretched his wings upon the breeze. Perhaps soon he would move to northern seas; but there was no hurry.

From somewhere in the evening sky came a distant sound, a forlorn lonely song, that was the voice of an arctic tern. She was the last of a flock of nine adolescents from one of the terneries in the Outer Hebrides. Soon the members of her flock had been lost on the great migration. Three had travelled no farther on their southern journey than the Bay of Biscay where storms had proved too much for their young wings. A male had dropped in the feeble hot airs of the equator. Another had been

105

snatched by a lanner falcon's claw. A black-point shark had taken the sixth as the tired flock rested too long on becalmed waters in the Bight of Benin. The last two had been victims of screaming snows less than fifty miles from the ice shelf. Only this female, Kilda, from a season's entire progeny, had reached Antarctica. She had looked to the adults of Drygalski Island to guide her through the summer months she had spent there; but now they had flown, had disappeared among the blizzards she feared. The last of the nine, she waited above the deserted ice-shores as she chased the fading Antarctic sun. Now, late March, was the time to return to the Scottish Isles. She was testing the air and calling with a diminishing hope that other terns might hear her. Sea-swallow followed the direction of the female's song, and his fatigue was forgotten. He searched the space above him and there he saw her. Leaving Greyback gliding across the shelf he curved upwards without for a moment losing sight of the distant female. Then his own voice burst out, calling to her, and it seemed his purpose had crystallised up there in the Antarctic sky.

Twenty feet apart the two terns circled. A sound which Sea-swallow had not heard for almost a year crossed the gap between them; 'kik-kik', and he knew, at least, that he was welcome and that the female wanted him close to her. He looked beneath to where the albatross flew. He sang out again and again, but Greyback continued to soar, apparently ignoring the tern's strident call. At last, inevitably, Sea-swallow and Kilda sloped their wings sunward and came about in a long sweep towards the north. Several times the male spiralled and looked back at the ice floes; but the albatross had gone without intruding upon his lost companion's flight with the silver female.

Greyback understood that the young tern would not come back. He flung his great wings against the breeze, and rushed away from the sea, skating across the gathering shadows of the drifts. A new loneliness travelled with him; but he did not understand its cause.

Antarctica fell beneath the scarlet-gold of dusk. Far beyond the banked teeth of ice-wrapped mountains a fading shape dropped towards the night.

PART THREE

Sea-swallow's return

ONE

Eight thousand feet above sea-level there was silence. Cold fingers of air sneaked through the feathers of the two arctic terns but it did not chill them. From where they hung the waves beneath were mere specks and all water motion was lost; the ocean lay in an infinite curl, the crystal smooth face of a giant waste, harmless and still; but they knew it was an illusion. At their starboard wings reared another expanse, the Cape veldt of Africa with the brown and gold burn marks of months beneath the sun.

The crossing of the southern seas had not been easy. They had fed on tiny fish borne on the cold-water currents. They had skimmed down from the spray-filled sky and had plunged into green walls where fish shoals swam. They had followed the sun where it showed through in seaward-slanting beams between cloud fronts. Hail had fallen in swarms of noise and had flattened the crisp edges of waves, robbing the two travellers of the draughts they needed for stable low-altitude flight. Bravely they flew on, strengthened by each other's company, while instinct and memory told them of northern lands, of their destination in time and space and purpose.

In the nights that followed they curved away from the star-crowds of Centaurus and travelled up the shores of Africa towards Jupiter and Saturn, the brightest bodies in the northern sky. They were not alone. Bitterns and night herons formed slowly waving lines above the coast. Swallows and martins flew in vast flocks as dark as locust swarms. Lanner falcons hunted in pairs, confused rather than aided by the concentration of their prey. Common and little terns, fresh from a season down the coast as far as the Cape of Good Hope, flew easily through the warm air, knowing that it would not be long before they met the first cool draughts of the northern ocean. Arctic terns flew with them, overtaking the slower-moving flocks, the freshening memory of Europe spurring them on.

Very few migrants paused to feed, for they had stored enough energy from a season's fishing upon the summer seas. Small groups broke away from the main body of the flocks and travelled to the coast, where the stale waters of a mud delta dampened their throats. Some managed to catch up with their friends, though most travelled on alone, and some lay down their wings upon the sun-hot mud, among the shadows of vultures. Even when individuals were lost from their flocks the leaders did not pause. Their instinct warned them that to wait too long here in the tropics could mean that none might reach the trade winds which would guide them to temperate seas. The strong ones had a single duty to those that followed: to lead them home.

Disorientated by a tropical squall Sea-swallow and Kilda travelled far out over the ocean. There they met their greatest threat.

On the fifteen degree latitude south of the equator a cyclone was born. At first it was a small area of ruffled

112

ocean, where the surface was warm, and a straggling patch of cloud was beginning to condense into a more sinister form. Within an hour it was a tightening ring of vapour starting to twist, throwing off trailing clusters of cloud at its edge.

Slowly the young hurricane moved westwards, growing in power with every minute, until by nightfall it had a diameter of a hundred miles. By the following dawn it had doubled its size and had changed course, now cutting north, lifting the deep Atlantic in its passage. In another twelve hours it had completely 'recurved' and was heading south-east, spinning wildly, obliterating the sun from thousands of square miles of heaving ocean.

The terns had rested on the sea, sleepless through the night, unable to fold head under wing because of the oppressive danger building around them. Soon after dusk they had watched the stars fade and slip slowly into hiding behind a thickening blanket of mist. The tide surged about them with long powerful swells, lifting them and passing swiftly by, poised to break into violence.

A western arm of the hurricane was closing upon the birds, enclosing them, and any other luckless creature that lay in its sweep, and carrying them towards the main body of cloud, hidden out in the night. Urgently the terns flew. Sea-swallow, remembering how the albatross had aided him, led Kilda along the steep-walled valleys between the waves, avoiding the main force of the wind. Tunnels of spray swung around them so that the only escape was to fly their length and burst clear through curling walls of water into the anger of the storm. Twice Kilda was flung into the sea. Both times she managed to lift her drenched body away before a wave collapsed on

113

the spot where she had fallen. The sea danced against the wind, hurling itself towards the frail bird-forms frantically beating amongst the chaos.

The birds climbed away from the sea, lifting themselves into the tremendous weight of rain pushing down at their backs and wings. Electricity stung at their bodies while the hurricane glowed with its own energy, ugly as the ocean beneath. They could neither see nor hear each other as they dragged themselves into the thunderclouds. Sea-swallow's wings swept at the air until, just as it seemed that he would never reach sanctuary, the noise began to fade and he was flying through cloud no thicker than a moorland mist. Then this too was gone and he was suddenly drenched in sunlight, glistening droplets of water falling from his tail streamers back into the hungry jaws of the cyclone. But Kilda was not with him. He dropped back down into the hurricane's misty limits, where a great roar met him. A blast of air cast him back up into clear sky. He circled, calling frantically, his voice ripped away on the cruel wind. The hurricane growled its reply, and bird-like wisps of vapour broke from the cloud-bulk to give him false hope. One beat of his wings and he was thrown a mile across the sky on powerful spinning gusts. The hurricane was holding much of the heat which would otherwise have lifted and held him effortlessly at high altitude. Now the wind tore about him, ruffling his streamlined feathers and plucking him down towards the cloud, where there was only certain death in the foaming sea. He dropped lower, his breast and wing muscles flexing wildly as he struggled for stability. A tiny glimmer of silver streaked across the cloud beneath him. He chased it for a moment until he realised that it was not Kilda but a shower of spray

114

thrown from the bucking storm.

Downwind: if the female was alive she would have been carried downwind. Sea-swallow again clawed himself across the sky. The air quivered with thunder and, as he flew lower, shock-waves rushed up and enveloped him, swinging and tumbling his fragile body, mocking his puny effort. As the turbulence passed he dropped farther. Now he was reading the shifting map of the cyclone. Here the air rolled constantly, and without shocks, beneath his wings. He called but could not hear his own voice. All he had was his strength and his eyes, searching the chaotic maze of vapour and water that was flung around him. He was above a mile-long hill of smooth cloud, as white as avalanching snow. It mirrored the sun and dazzled him. He turned east, away from the glare and towards a hole which dropped deep into the storm, its walls marked by cascades of luminous haze.

A torrent of rain spilled like a waterfall across his back. In a moment he was clear and weaving amongst pillars that towered for hundreds of feet into blizzards of ice, golden and salmon-pink against the sun.

Then Sea-swallow was above the hurricane's eye, a calm patch of dense moist air twenty-five miles across. Beneath him the Atlantic lay peaceful and tempting, untroubled by the surrounding cylinder of grey-black storm. At the eye's centre a rush of heat lifted him for a thousand feet, and would have carried him far higher if he had allowed. But a sound made him halt his ascent; a feeble high-pitched note from far down in the eye, a bird sound. Kilda was clear and he had found her. She rose up to him on the hot draught. After a brief mid-air touch of their bills, a snatched cry of delight and song, they planed up towards the motionless heights and out over the remainder of the eye until they were above the northern reaches of the hurricane, now alight with the smouldering reds of evening.

For an hour they hurtled across the waning hearth of the sky. They had taken a full day of continuous flying to reach this far and still ahead of them was the night, and over three hundred miles of cyclone. Instinct told them that they must continue flying north. The star twins in Gemini had set and were lost for navigational purposes, but Hydra's fine lines guided them through equatorial skies. Now Sea-swallow and Kilda could sustain each other until the ocean's violence was leashed again.

Weary, the two young birds beat through the humid airs of the tropics. Unseen, a mile above coastal mangrove swamps, they glided in the half-light of a new day while they watched for movement against the brightening panorama of Africa.

For a day they flew west along the coast, the steep yellow beaches of Ghana rolling beneath them, but they did not pause for fear of fishing boats, and nets which hung from poles in the sand, bone-hard in the sun. By nightfall they had reached the estuary of the river Volta. Where fresh water met the tide, a smouldering carpet of phosphorescent plankton was laid out in long lines a mile beyond the river mouth, breaking the sea into a patchwork of silver fragments.

Throughout the night the terns drifted upon the estuary waters. The drought-stricken river crept into the mid-Atlantic, a stagnant shadow of what it would be when the monsoons came. From the south came the grumbling of the sea-shore, of breakers pounding their relentless strength upon the sand. The ocean breeze did not reach far along the river, and palms stood along the shores like rows of torn umbrellas awaiting another blazing day. To the north the silent presence of Africa opened beyond the moon-silvered waters, a rising heap of terrain.

The scent of forest and heat, and of the plains of low-land Ghana, drifted down river and settled upon their feathers. Lizards scuttered along the shore while owls and bats slunk through the shadows. Many eyes winked from the darkness, watching the slow-running river. Sea-swallow felt Kilda's head nudge and rest against his shoulder. Antarctica and Scotland were fading in his memory, like a dream that he wanted to recapture with the sleeping female at his side.

A soft rushing sound whispered across the plain. Upon the wind hung the far away screech of a crater eagle. This sound was hardly heard, and yet it was louder than the breeze on which it was borne. Dawn singed across the east; a scarlet glow became, in minutes, a streaming orange incandescence too bright to look at. The terns, both awake, silently paddled at the river's feeble flow while day-light revealed the shrunken estuary. Every-where was tainted with the red of the iron-rich earth. The early light deepened the effect, and only the palms stood out a dull green against the fiery backdrop.

Slowly the colours brightened and the vivid red faded to rust. Maize plantations spread along the river shores, sparse but yellow-green, defiant to the sun. Village huts stood far back from the mud flats, with whispers of blue smoke still rising from night fires. Shabby-coated cattle, ribs and shoulders protruding from hanging folds of flesh, meandered with heads lowered, along the river banks. Only termites seemed successful here on the

117

plains. Their mound dwellings, built from the red earth, sprawled across the landscape, some larger than the homes of men.

A frog croaked from the sluggish waters close into the bank, and a mamba slithered through the reeds, gone in a writhing turn of glossy black. The two birds saw the motion and felt danger in this place. Quietly they lofted their wings and stole up into the damp air. Few eyes saw them pass high above the estuary, close together, and drift far out over the airy relief of the Atlantic.

TWO

Above the ocean, somewhere off Africa, two separate pairs of birds were flying more than a mile away from the western sands. Kilda and Sea-swallow had formed a pair-bond which their shared migration across the southern seas had intensified. But the other pair, not far behind the first, though still out of sight, possessed a different kind of bond, one which had stood the test of many shared journeys.

It was the last day of April and the old common tern had never felt so tired, so worn by endless flight. He was already master of twenty-two migrations and he was now on the return journey of his twenty-third; but his head was held more askew than usual and his neck hurt. Neither was the vision in his one good eye as sharp as it had once been. He felt the miles slide painfully beneath his wings. Shocksilver, up ahead, was still the graceful silver bird, though he too was not young; but he always possessed his sense of strength, his indomitable purpose. He was continuously alert to his surroundings, forever watching, forever leading. Hawkwind could only follow the strong arctic tern. It was almost habit; they had been together for so long.

The skies of the African flyway were crowded with migrating flocks. Day and night they passed with haste at their wings and breath for nothing more than to fill hot lungs to speed their home-bound voyage. There was nothing to tempt them to remain here in Africa. They heard the cries of falcons above the dusty terrain; there was no promise of rain to turn parched grasslands into marsh, no gluts of fish by island reefs; only the sun, or the star-mapped nights, showing the way to the north. They flew again towards their ancestral homes and they filled the air with sheets of wings, an unstoppable tide of life washing towards Europe.

A flock of sandwich terns disappeared in the northern sky. Shocksilver watched them go. He seemed more alert than usual. He flew without song, planing, listening, waiting, with Hawkwind silent at his tail. Together they eased their left wings down and pushed themselves in a slow curve away from Africa. Then it happened: out over the sea came a twinned flash in the afternoon sun, and a call, 'keeray', cutting through the sky, a voice which both Shocksilver and the common tern understood. The call faded as the two birds canted their pinions and swooped. Ahead of them Sea-swallow and Kilda came away from the western glare. In a moment Hawkwind was transformed. His fatigue was gone. He had overtaken Shocksilver, his head pushed forward as he ignored the pain it caused him. He clawed the air as he thrust in rapid ascent, his tail held in a narrow needle. His wings fell flat against his body while momentum drove him upward, like a comet firing across space.

Now they were all climbing, Sea-swallow and the female, Shocksilver and the common tern, almost touching as they rose into the vault of an empty sky. A fierce

120

oxygen-tingle ran along their spines while their air speed increased still more. Hawkwind threw himself above the others; five thousand feet, six thousand, seven, they levelled and turned about, head into wind. In the distance beneath they picked out the shapes of other flocks, though they could not be certain, for at that altitude the tiny forms of birds were camouflaged against the continuous firework-flash of the foaming sea. Hawkwind's shoulders eased forward, his tail hooked down, spread to the draught. The arctics watched him go while for a second longer they held themselves aloft in the turbulence. Then they too curled into a dive, four hundred feet behind Hawkwind. Their streamlined bodies made barely a hiss as they fell, and for half a minute the sea revolved beneath them, the bursts of foam growing into pools and long, broken lines. Together they stretched trembling wings to slow their fall . . . There, above the hot African tide, the contentment and longing of four individuals had merged and in the fusion it had grown.

Together now the four terns probed northwards, away from the heavy airs of the tropics. The temperate Atlantic rolled ahead and the skies were alive with a thousand wings and a thousand songs. The last haul was punishing to taut muscles. Heat was replaced by exhaustion, but the strong came through. The sun was approaching the Crab, and Ursa Major was high above Europe. Polaris had risen. Sea-swallow was excited now; his memory told him that he was approaching the end of his fantastic migration; he was almost home. The ocean slid cold beneath him and the wind was cool in his throat. In the Bay of Biscay he was frightened by ships. He drew up close to Kilda as he remembered the menace of men's

121

machines: the pain at his wings was gone, the female was there, crescent white before his eyes.

The Bay was crossed and the coast became wilder, more pitted by reefs and rocks and spray. North; Shock-silver beat relentlessly towards the north. There were fewer than a thousand miles to go; only the English Channel to cross and then the length of the west coast of Britain. They could follow the fish shoals all the way, and the prevailing wind would guide them inevitably to Scotland.

The Channel slept, allowed them across without further struggle. The sunlit coast of Cornwall humped from the sea. They watched it grow before them and now they were all excited; even Hawkwind beat with renewed strength. The migrants had returned; summer was ripening in the north.

THREE

James, the boy of the *Firedragon* incident, was fishing from the quayside beneath 'Cliff-Edge'. He had not forgotten the oil-tanker and the black tides, and the thousands of poisoned birds that he knew had died; but at least the sea was blue again and the fish were returning. Dark stains still appeared on the sands of Tregale beach although it was eighteen months since the tanker explosion. James looked out across the bay where herring gulls were diving upon a fish shoal. There were not so many birds as there used to be but the boy could not imagine greater beauty than this, his home, despite the lingering stains of oil.

A bird among the gulls caught his attention. It was a tern, an old one with frayed feathers and a crooked neck. As he watched, the tern rose away from the screeching gulls and the boy could see three other fork-tailed birds climbing behind the first. James jumped up, almost treading on his fishing rod. His stare was fixed upon the silver birds. As the small flock came closer the boy's expression changed. At first it was wonder, a questioning uncertainty, with his face creased in his effort to see the birds more clearly. Then his eyes opened wide and his

123

inquisitive hope had become delight. His thoughts raced, slipping back to a grey October morning when the only beauty he could see in the world was a tiny silver shape in the sky: the tern he had saved and released. One word came from his lips – 'Sea-swallow'.

The flock now circled above him. He saw how incomplete were the text-book descriptions of terns. The birds were more than 'translucent against a bright sky', they were shimmering like raindrops in the sun; they were more than 'hawk-swallow shaped', with their delicate fingering feathers spread on the air. And their voices were not only 'strident and piercing', but perfectly blended with the sounds of a Cornish sea: rhythmic and purposeful, far more graceful than the background row of gull sounds. How many books about sea birds he had read since that cold October, and yet none of them had captured the vision of the terns' perfect flight.

The flock was beginning to fly out of the bay. James had an idea. He grabbed a strip of mackerel from his bait tin and held it in an upraised hand. Almost immediately the tern nearest him stooped, coming to rest in a hover twenty feet above the trembling boy. Two gulls were screeching and rapidly approaching from the sea. The tern hesitated, his wings vibrating as he held himself in a kestrel-steady poise. For a moment it seemed to James that his stare and the bird's had met. Sea-swallow was wary, anxious, finally trusting the upheld gift and its bearer. Then in a blur of wings the mackerel was snatched from the boy's hand. The fish was immediately gulped down. 'Keeray', called Sea-swallow as he flew beyond the cliffs towards Kilda and the others.

James watched him go, thought of holding up another strip of mackerel but did not do so. The moment had gone and could not be repeated. He was certain that the bird was in fact Sea-swallow. He also knew of the colossal migration to and from Antarctica, a place which James himself could barely even imagine. And yet he had made it possible by rescuing the tern, the only one he had managed to save from the *Firedragon* oil, and setting him free when he had recovered.

There was Sea-swallow's final 'keeray', and James interpreted the sound as the bird's thanks for what had happened over a year ago. 'They won't believe me at home', thought James; but he did not really care.

FOUR

A summer gale was blowing from the south. It was warm though the sky was dull and filled with slanting rain. The Scottish cliffs were dark and malevolent; white ribbons of waves were torn into tatters of spray which scattered over the rocks in a tumult of noise. Shocksilver led his flock slightly across the wind so that they travelled almost due east between Loch Eriboll and the Kyle of Seals.

For seventeen miles of cliff and foam the terns had been slowing down. Now the leader paused above the grasping tide-claw. Beneath him Sea-swallow hovered, his wings slashing the rain into a mist. Here, in this wild fragment of the north, his migration lust was dimmed. Sea-swallow banked to bring the pounding breakers into view — the tide was never still — but it had ceased to hold any fear for him, with all its great motion.

A porpoise school, also seeking shelter beneath the cliffs, could be seen a little way beyond the breakers. Dark backs thrust through shallow waters into driving rain. Foam rose and fell about them.

The wind was moderating now. As the small flock approached the estuary of the river Hope they could see deep into the clear water where wrasse and pollack swam above colonies of mussels. Anemones and corals bloomed like flowers from fields of kelp and wrack: the summer swarms littered the shore-line where, three months earlier, bare rock had lain smeared with icy surf.

The sun burst through thinning cloud and the gale was over. Within minutes the sky was crowded with birds. They burst from the crevices in cliffs, from marram grass and sand-dunes. Gulls winged swiftly out to sea in search of victims of the storm. A heron trod the edges of a rock pool, his stare working across the suddenly still water. Hooded crows spiralled above the cliffs at the edge of the moor, and gannets plunged upon a fish shoal at the river mouth.

Home. Home again after the struggles of migration, the exhausting months above the pitching reaches of the southern ocean and the heavy heat of the tropics. The two adolescent terns, Kilda and Sea-swallow, played on the breezes of the storm's last gusts. Shocksilver and the old tern dropped upon sand-eels in the shallows. Hawk-wind was tired, content only that he had managed to reach Scotland where he could rest through the weak heat of summer. He turned his good eye towards the shore where mounds of grass beckoned. With little strength left he glided and finally came to rest upon a clump of sea-thrift. Waves thrashed beneath him, but the noise came to him like music, like the voices of Kilda and the young male, full of memory and hope.

A thousand yards above, hidden against the last wisps of cloud, a peregrine falcon, with her young tiercel, soared and watched. Her huntress eyes had seen the approaching terns, themselves blinded by wind and spray, from many miles distant. She and the tiercel had shot steeply into the sky until they were camouflaged against high cloud. Now they turned and waited for the moment to close their wings and drop into the high-speed joy of a killing stoop.

Sea-swallow was uneasy. He swung around, observing the pearl-grey of Kilda's breast and the white of her under-wings; but not until it was too late did he see the danger. The female was relaxed, her head turned down as she watched for movements in the waves. Emerald-green bars of light winked from just below the surface where crustacea and fish fry trembled in a swirl of glittering sand. The tern's wings quivered and her tail spread open, maintaining her in a hover thirty feet clear of her targets. She could hear Sea-swallow's startled voice, a quick 'che-che-che-che', but in her excitement she ignored it for a second too long. Then the falcon kicked her out of the sky. A cloud of her own feathers followed her descent towards the waves. She tumbled over, unable to regain her balance, winded by the force of the falcon's attack.

'Gyake', the death-scream of the peregrine struck upon the wind. Again the falcon was swooping, grey-black talons spread out before her chest. Kilda was threshing upon the surface, desperately sucking air into her lungs as she turned to face the killer; but there was time only to cry her fear before a talon smashed into her neck. She felt an insurmountable power wrench her from the sea. For a moment she beat her wings at the enemy, but stopped when another talon bit into her chest.

The falcon rose in a staggering, strained way with the burden of Kilda's still shape clasped tightly to her belly. She had climbed twenty feet before Sea-swallow hit her. She spat at the frenzied scythe shape of Shocksilver whose wing-tips flicked at her eyes. She swept her hooked bill at him to frighten him off. She drew one talon free from Kilda's body so that she could bring this, her most powerful of weapons, to bear; but the terns had respect neither for her claw nor for her embittered voice.

The tiercel was stooping, manoeuvering his pinions fractions of an inch to alter the direction of his dive. Shocksilver saw him and banked away from the others. The tiercel came at him, slashing out with spread talons as the tern looped clear, robbing his attacker of initiative. 'Kee-kee', cried Hawkwind as he joined in the attack, his exhaustion forgotten.

Now both peregrines were climbing, flight suddenly difficult as all directions of escape were cut off by stabbing bills or a whiplash blow of a wing. Repeatedly they kicked out as the terns swooped around. For two thousand feet the spinning ball of rage rose above the cliffs. The falcon was tiring as wings slapped into her own, causing her to thrust harder to stop herself from falling beneath the rain of hatred. Simultaneously Hawkwind's bill lanced into her neck as Sea-swallow's shoulder hit hard into her right eye. If she was to escape without further harm her prize was lost and she, huntress supreme, was now the hunted. Her grip on Kilda's neck loosened and the falcon jerked clear, suddenly free, racing into the sky.

Apparently lifeless, Kilda's body fell like a discarded puppet and smacked into the sea where it lay sprawled on the broiling waters beneath a cliff. Sea-swallow hovered above her while flecks of spray pattered against his chest. But he did not feel the sea, or hear its relentless roar. He had eyes only for slight movements of his female's head as she struggled to breathe. The swell threw her upon a ledge where she came to rest with the tide foaming about her. Again her head moved and she opened her eyes, finding that she could still see. Her neck and chest hurt, and salt stung at a gash along her back. She could not recall falling from the falcon's grip, only the shock of the attack, though she still heard her friends' protective voices, incessant, louder than the sea. Another wave ran at her and pushed her higher on to the rock. When the foam had uncovered her face Kilda saw that she was not alone; and with the warmth of Sea-swallow's breast pushing at her shoulder the fear was gone.

The tiercel was in trouble. Shocksilver and Hawkwind tore at him, stabbing and shouting their battle-cries; but the common tern had climbed too high and he was feeling dizzy. For a second he tilted slightly away from the peregrine and exposed his blind side to attack. He felt himself shaking and trembling uncontrollably. The horizon sloped before him and he could not find the strength to bring his wings back to a level attitude. With a lurch the tiercel became anchor shaped and plummeted towards the unwary tern. A claw punched out, tearing two parallel lines of flesh from Hawkwind's neck. Then the peregrine was away, beating into the sanctuary of a power dive towards the earth, three thousand feet below.

The injured tern staggered back from the blow, reeling away, spiralling, while blood flushed from his twin wounds and streaked along his back. He still saw the horizon, tilted more than before, and there was a numbness along his right flank. Shocksilver appeared before him, silver feathers quivering, calling something that the common tern could not hear. Hawkwind broke out of his spiral descent and found the horizon steady again. He had lost a great deal of height. Shocksilver's starboard wing clipped against the side where Hawkwind still had feeling, and again they were turning, coming away from the

130

sea, until the mountain at the head of Loch Hope stood directly ahead; a giant final destination on the silent moorland. On the ledge far below Sea-swallow and Kilda watched the two gliding shapes. The female's head sagged as pain seared through her body. She could still hear the voices of her companions singing in her ears. Much later, in the twilight of evening, when Shocksilver alone returned, the voices still danced about her, although one had faded to almost nothing.

The mother-spirit of the Isles has been sleeping long enough. Her arms are the wind and soft-spoken tides of summer, closing together in cradling grasps and blue-green smothers of sea. Her substance is the success of seasons past, the souls of beings who have lived beneath her spell. Now she stirs, and already her message reaches across the ocean, for time is precious and there is much to be done. And from afar the migrants come to find the lands little different from how they were last year. The burns run in a tumble of water from the snow thaw on the hills rather than with autumn spates. In a river mouth a new bend has formed during winter floods; an ash has been uprooted and carried a mile from its birth to lie as a wind-bleached skeleton high above the waves where spring tides have set it down. But the rocks and the Isles still stand, and the sea still pulses its endless rhythm at the land's edge.

To these things the wanderers return; though death also waits. Silver flanks of sea-trout shine through moor-land waters to attract the osprey's vigil. Now there are more than salmon kelts or brown trout for the talon's grasp; stronger flesh to tear apart. And other hunters watch for the bounty borne on the south wind. Above all it seems the land cares for those who have remained faithful winter-long, those who did not run from the cold. Lean deer walk upon the hills to find new growth waiting there; the fox is fat at last. Cautiously, or insouciant, the migrants arrive.

PART FOUR

The silver king

ONE

As darkness fades into the misty light of early morning the sea is silent. A breeze blows softly from the heather and.ruffles out over the shallow waters. The tide is never still, but now it runs smoothly around the islands, surging along the rock and lapping over the beaches, caressing the sand. Violence has gone from the sea and is now no more than a bad memory of the year's earlier months. The bird colonies — the terneries, the puffins hidden in their peat burrows, even the skuas upon their moorland nests — are quiet far into the morning. A slow sweep of slate-grey wing betrays where a fulmar sits upon her single egg in a cliff crevice. Only the gulls seem not to be content to sit in morning peace within their territorial bounds. For them, to be on the wing, with quick eyes investigating every fine detail of the sea-shore, is the promise of full stomachs. To rest is to be hungry while others, more diligent and alert, find food as the concealing shrouds of darkness unfold.

Nothing moves on the surface of the sea. Cumulus clouds grow from the horizon and stand serene and white, with no threat of rain or storm. The eastern sky is not yet too bright to watch, and the night still clings to

135

the shadows, where nesting birds sleep, safe from the questing eyes of gulls. No sounds but the tide's low gurgle or the far off cry of a waking curlew disturb the peace, and even these sounds are part of the mood of this becalmed fringe of the north-eastern Atlantic.

Three terns, close together, approach the sea. They beat steadily through the slight breeze and close with the beach. At once they are both wary and watchful, though the male who leads them appears sure of his direction. Two green islands bar their way. They move over the sand and rise above the grass, gliding on the gentle sun-draught. No calls of abuse meet them, no exclamations to protect territory, no enemy, rising on dark wings, to usher them once again into battle. Within minutes of their arrival the terns are relaxed. Sea-swallow, with the female at his side, comes to rest upon a hillock which offers a view in all directions. To seaward only the white flash of a herring gull's wings marks the heat haze. North-east from where he stands a chain of islands curls around the coast and terminates with the rocky mound of Auk Island. To the south lie the tidal sands of Tongue Bay and the Kyle of Seals. But Shocksilver does not land. He circles and climbs, suddenly alone on the breeze. He has been alone here before; he still remembers the sound of the gun and the smell of the female's blood.

Leaving the two young ones on the island the silver tern flies west from the Kyle of Seals and up over the moorland. He drops across a slope towards the omni-present heights of Ben Hope. Soon he comes to a place at the edge of the long loch. There is nothing there but green shoots of new heather. He settles and stands alone upon the naked peat. His head turns down and his stare becomes fixed upon an empty space, as if he sees some-

136

thing which is invisible to all but himself. The wind moans softly overhead though it barely penetrates between the hills. It is a voice, rising and falling from a point far above. It belongs to the moorland spirit, to mountains at the sea's edge, where life is one with death; where, for Shocksilver at least, Nightwing still flies.

It is June and the terns explore the kyle and surrounding moorland, pausing at several sandy areas of the coast that are secluded and yet open to the ocean sky. A short distance over the heather at the southern end of the kyle lies a chain of three lochs beneath the giant peaks of Ben Loyal. Here they hunt for trout and salmon fry, but they are uncomfortable near the restricting rock walls, and remain ever alert for harriers and falcons that steal in, on silent wings, low to the camouflaging terrain. The three birds fly the lengths of the Sister rivers to where the peaty streams meet and mingle upon the sands of Torrisdale Bay. Many sheltered pockets in the dunes attract them, or grassy ledges above the pounding tide; but each night Shocksilver leads them back to the islands of the kyle.

Isolated from the mainland by a narrow race of water, the most southerly island offers an ideal environment for a ternery. There is grass for nests, and shell-sand on almost every shore. Eels and flatfish abound at the surf's edge, and there is no shortage of moths and sedge-fly on calm evenings. At night the dwellings of men show as pinpoints of light and etch narrow silver streaks across the face of the kyle, but they are far off, presenting no menace, and there is the open sea to the north, with its promise of escape.

Altogether there are now more than two dozen pairs of

arctic terns assembled on the Rabbit Isles. It is nesting time and the scrapes and hollows are densely packed on the most favourable sights. Because the northern calm will not be long-lived the season demands urgency. The marriage of the terns is swift, though faithful. Vociferous courtship displays accompany territorial confrontation. Birds that have travelled together from Antarctica become rivals, or companions closer than before.

Kilda's belly strokes the surface of Loch Loyal and draws a fork of sun-shot water behind her tail. Sea-swallow slips along at her side, imitating her flight as perfectly as a shadow. His rhythm breaks so that on the upstroke the point of his starboard wing brushes at her breast, where water droplets lie. He arches his body and slows his speed, allowing the female to drift beneath him. Imperceptibly she bows her wings so that she rises and her tail streamers brush across his face. Gently he pecks at her and they are held by the trailing silver edge of her body as they glide, before both birds pull in their shoulders and drop down towards the shortening shadows of morning.

They soar through the mountain passage and come above the southern end of the kyle. The isles of Tongue Bay gradually lift into view beyond the bridge and Fortress Point. A salmon leaps beneath them, its lilac flank flashing in a turn of whirring fins. Somehow it has escaped the nets. Behind the leaper a shoal of fry rush across the surface in sudden terror. Sea-swallow collapses into a dive, his target already chosen from the synchronised mass of twinkling life.

Before Kilda has circled once the male is again at her side, bearing his silver gift. Her stare moves from the fish in his grasp to the graceful power of his body, and lingers

138

there. Together they rise while a new excitement trembles within them. It flows gently. One day it will course and burst within and between them until it becomes their final purpose; but not for another year will the young pair breed – at two years of age they are still too young. Now they must prove the loyalty of their union, for they must pair for life. If next year they are still together, if they survive the rigours of another 25,000-mile migration, then they will nest. In the meantime they learn from other pairs. They watch the fish-dances and the mating flights. Sea-swallow looks to the female, who looks to him, and they are both excited.

Peace comes again with the midnight dusk, a wide orange band in the north-west stretching and fading across the sky to die finally in deep crimson on the east. The sea-birds quieten down but do not sleep. Some beat silently from mainland to island, their undersides a deeper red than the sky. A polished-calm ocean moves lazily to the moon's invisible pull, and the wind is hardly more than a draught in an island crag, or the touch of a breeze at the tide's edge. The sea campion and marram does not move, while isles and rocks lie off-shore like stranded whales or conning towers of submarines.

Later, when colour has gone from sea and sky, the journey of the sun is marked by a pale northern glow, and at last the only airborne wings are those of bats and moths above trees and moor at the kyle's edge.

A rank smell of nesting fulmars wafts among the dunes with the tang of summer growth, of milkwort and mayweed, of acid peat beneath a carpet of fresh heather and flowering heath; though only the heavy odour of fulmar and a rotting crab upon the beach can be distinguished from the finer scents of the shore.

139

The tide slows its ebb and sluices back in a gurgling rush between the kyle and the ternery. The wind comes up from the open sea and picks wavelets from the calm. In the early hours of the morning the aura of dawn swells and colour returns. The exploding grenade of bird-song climbs into the air faster than the sun. Gulls and kittiwakes climb on the new breeze while a heron's ghostly silhouette sweeps towards a sandy creek at the kyle's southern end, where sea-trout enter the peaty river.

Everything has its time and place. Now the sea-board is the home of the birds; the rivers belong to the salmon, while sundew and marsh orchids peep above the moorland carpet that all too soon will be a blaze of purpling heather. And then the flowering will be over and dark salmon kelts will turn away from the redds and run to sea. Where the terns now sit to hatch their eggs, grey seals will give birth to their pups. The nights will live with the sounds of hail and spray, and the north wind will carry shearwaters and petrels closer off-shore. The channels between the isles will be the migration routes of baleen whales and basking sharks. All too soon the northern hemisphere will tilt away from the sun.

Men have not marked much that happens here; it is Europe's last wilderness before the Atlantic wastes.

TWO

Stars reflected from the wavelets of the kyle in a mobile blue-white scatter, undimmed by the brighter light of the moon which had not yet risen above the mainland hills. The island colony had long since been silent. A brooding voice, a shuffle in the sand or the snap of popping wrack were the only sounds to betray the presence of terns at their nests. Owl song, muffled by leaves of birch and ash, came from the woods at the kyle's edge, and a seal's gargling snore gave rhythm to the night. A westerly promised fair weather for the day to come. But alone on bare rock above the dunes where the tern flock had collected, Shocksilver could not sleep. He was motionless though alert, his eyes shining as brightly as the sea's surface, his attitude wary of a danger that he sensed was waiting out in the night, biding its time.

At Kilda's side Sea-swallow was also awake, anxious for dawn to streak the eastern sky so that the threat might be exposed. From beneath many sleeping females came the stirring of shell-protected life. Shocksilver might have sensed that it was this same nurtured life that drew danger towards the colony. A pair of wings, dark as the night, flapped low to the waves. The bird they carried

141

was an arctic skua. Twice Shocksilver heard the wings orbit the island, and then, with its malignant presence, the skua soared away upon the breeze.

Quietly night faded until a clear purple canopy lit an empty sea. Not until sunrise did birds fly across the waters of the kyle.

Chestnut breasts flickered as a flock of dotterels flew down from the mountains while, a mile behind, a harrier's buff wings beat in pursuit. A rabbit's squeal stabbed from the moorland as a stoat's sharp teeth met their target. Unseen, somewhere amongst the waves to the north, the arctic skuas waited, their mumbling chatter rising and falling like the throbbing tone of a windless sea: the day of the hunter had begun.

Skubill, the Great Skua, opened his eyes and stretched his stiff neck as wings brushed overhead. He watched as his flock grew and gathered around. The waves lifted him so that a dull shoulder of island-scattered shoreline came beneath his stare. His belly grumbled for attention while a young female crooned at his side, until his driving bill drew blood from her neck to dull her mistimed amour. Hunger prevailed.

Farther to the north a trawler fleet made its way towards the Orkney fishing banks. The undersides of gulls turned orange against the sun, signalling to the skua flock, in the language of scavengers, the message of food.

Noonday passed and the summer wind blew, riffling across the shallow waters. Shocksilver slid above the channel between mainland and island where the tide raced and curled. Sea-swallow followed him, continuously scanning the northern sky where as yet there was little movement. Two black-headed gulls were arguing over the remains of a mussel shell upon the beach. Kilda

142

glanced skyward towards the two spiralling males. Her desire to be with them, to join with their majestic flight, was intense, and she also was sensitive to the threat that hung like death on the air.

An adolescent moved up to guard Shocksilver's port flank. So far there had been no commands, merely united fear, or wariness; preparation for an ordeal that was to follow. The three together tilted their wings and swung away from the north, back towards the island. Two more males climbed up to meet them and manouvred easily into formation. Shocksilver hooked clear and flew above them, gradually drawing away until they lost sight of him on the far side of the island; but out over the ocean they saw the dark scattered pattern of their enemy.

The arctic skuas had not had a good day with the fishing fleet. Gulls had beaten them to the most plentiful sites. Now, with eggs and fledglings rather than fish on their minds, they swarmed and rode towards the coast. As they approached the kyle they bunched together in a bow formation, Skubill, the Great Skua, out in front, while the defence calls of nesting birds met their ears: sweet music leading them to the feast.

There were now a dozen terns airborne. The females remained crouched and silent upon the sand. Sea-swallow directed his flock east, away from the island, and then north to meet the skuas over the sea. A fish shoal moved beneath him, and without hesitation he plunged. Others dropped about him, each sending up the message of food in a spout of white foam. The bursts of movement caught the skuas' attention and held it long enough to make them swerve away from the island and pursue the decoy flight.

Shocksilver drifted above them, soaring like a buzzard.

143

His underwings flashed and Sea-swallow rose up towards him. They needed altitude. Height was speed in
free-fall: something that the skuas could not match.

Far down the kyle a flock of oystercatchers paused in
their feeding as they waded amongst the ebbing waters.
They looked out to sea, to where the battle cries of skuas
and terns burst forth, frightening even at that distance,
building as the conflict progressed, as the many dark
wings fluttered and bore down upon the pale shapes.
Even the seals, lazing away the afternoon upon the sand-
bars, cast baleful stares in the sea's direction.

Shocksilver and the young male waited high above,
like generals choosing where best to deploy their greatest
force. Already the terns were out-numbered, but there
was confusion as the skuas searched for fish. The females
upon the beach remained quiet. A tern came out of the
waves with a sand-eel held crosswise in his bill. Immediately, even before the water had stopped running from
his wings, he was surrounded, with no space for him to
use his speed.

He was thrown into the sea by his enemy, and in falling
he was finished. The skuas clawed and tore at him. They
took his fish, but it was not enough. They held him
suspended by his wingtips above the sea while Skubill
tasted the blood of his chest. His life was not enough, nor
his flesh. After less than a minute the skuas left him as a
bedraggled pulp of bloody feathers, and then they rose
into the sky, crazed, their beaks and faces red with their
carnage. Their formation spelt hunger and murder and
death; their only master was Skubill, for he led them to
what they needed. No less powerful bird could stand
against them. The tern they had destroyed had done no
more than delay them, giving the nesting females on the

144

island more time to gather their chicks beneath them. They were a rogue-killer pack and now they regrouped and turned towards the beach colony where their real prize lay, hidden beneath the breasts and wings of brooding hens.

Three hundred feet above them the two silver terns planed. The remainder of the tern flock were fleeing back to the island where, as individuals they could stand and guard their nests. There was no fear in Shocksilver, or in Sea-swallow. Perhaps also there was no hate; but they had their shared presence and their united strength. And what they had to do was necessary. They could not allow the skuas to reach the island. Together they screeched their offence calls, 'kee-che-che-che', and pulled in their wings. Side by side the twinned silver punch fell seaward.

Almost too fast to see they stooped through the midst of the skuas. Shocksilver staggered as his left wing thudded against his enemy; but Skubill merely flinched. The old tern became a cross in the sky, the sun glancing from his out-spread wings. Skubill could not resist his beauty, his silver-covered flesh, his injured body beginning to falter, to stumble in the air. The Great Skua swerved, his eyes fixed on his new quest; but although Shocksilver was injured, he knew what he was doing. Even as he seemed to be losing control he was watching the skuas turn towards him, away from the island once again.

The carrion birds swooped towards Shocksilver, but before they could force him down into the sea where they could use their weight to defeat him, Sea-swallow was at their backs, his wings sweeping out like blades.

Suddenly the battle initiative was changing. The tern flock was returning to face the skuas, fresh courage

145

seeded among them by the old tern's actions. But they were nothing; in minutes they could be swept aside.

Again Shocksilver staggered. He flapped wildly as if struggling for purchase on the air. For an instant he appeared to have succeeded but then his left wing drooped, as if smashed, useless. He spiralled beneath the skuas and dropped gracelessly to the sea. In a heap he crashed down and flayed foam into the air. After a few moments he was still, his wings spread as if in defeat or death. It was irresistible to Skubill whose bowed wings cast a dark shadow across the place where Shocksilver lay. Above him was his flock, uncertain now as a rain of terns whipped through them. Momentarily the Great Skua hesitated, although the sight of Shocksilver's body drew him inevitably down.

The silver tern exploded from the sea, driving his bill deep into the vulnerable underside above him. He felt the skua recoil with a quick inhalation of breath, but then claws grasped at his shoulders and he was wrenched by an overwhelming strength. Together the two birds fell into the sea where the skua's greater weight forced Shocksilver beneath the surface. The dark bird rose, his body curved, glistening like his eyes with the final joyful moments of victory. It was no longer a decoy. Shocksilver lay helpless on the tide, his head clamped in the skua's beak. He had barely the strength or sense to hold his feet raised to protect his belly, or to open his bill to form a gaping red gash of fury and delay Skubill for as long as possible; before the savage vengeance of Seaswallow came to his aid. And yet the chance had almost gone and unless he could fight now the skuas would make a bloody end to the day.

146

Now Sea-swallow is plummeting from the sky, alone and fierce, his pinion-tips exposed like daggers. In a blur another tern draws up at his side. It is Kilda. They swoop above the waves and fire along side by side. Their wings slap upon the water, for there is no more time to climb and they hug the shifting contours of the sea, summoning all the power they possess for their shared purpose.

Releasing Shocksilver, the skua spins around as he hears the approaching terns. In that instant Shocksilver drives himself up, stabbing into the dark chest above him, thrusting with the spear of his bill. Even as Kilda and Sea-swallow throw themselves at him the skua lowers his head and gasps in air that is to freeze into a shriek, to signal the end. As she passes, Kilda lunges down, the blow of the impact coming as a flash across her eyes.

A screeching sweeps the sky, reverberating like waves in the confines of a cave. When it stops the skuas are once again a disordered band rushing away from the kyle while Sea-swallow and the others give chase. Skubill flops down, his last breath breaking in a stream of bubbles upon the surface. Not far away another body rides across the wall of a swell. It is the silver arctic tern, surrounded by a halo of foam from his last struggles, his anger and his mighty presence ultimately vanquished. In the minutes that pass he does not move to give fresh hope to those eyes that had watched him fall. His body moves to the sea's motion, and as the mark of foam dissolves, the tide carries him towards deep water beyond the reefs; his secrets are lost to all but the strongest of his kind. The skua he had killed in his final, fighting moments travels with him. At last, in death, the enemies end their feud and give back their matter to the Atlantic which had served them both.

THREE

Far, far up in the sky the silver tern soars, one with the night. He banks until his belly is facing the glow of dawn, still young in the east. He has been here since dusk, half a mile or more above the black bowl of the sea, skating across the darkness. Soon he will have to go — he knows that — for the wind is losing its warmth and the great flocks have been gone for many weeks; but there is not a strong wish within him to leave, to put the Scottish hills at his tail; and the cliffs where he has known so much.

Sunlight streams through the mountains, shining apricot across the sea and casting the shore into deep shadows. The tern cuts inland for one last glimpse of the moor. It is quiet now, the harriers low to the heather or still asleep in their rocky eyries; though more than the silence draws him here towards the still mirror of the loch.

His wing-tips cant slightly upwards. Gracefully, the breeze a gentle hiss at his pinions' edge, he descends across the silver waters. A stag on the western shore glances skyward, a snort of vapour streaming from his nostrils. The tern sees the sudden movement of antlers and in ten wingbeats he has gone, swerving amongst the

148

birch trees and pines of the far hills. A mile up the loch he is back over the water, stroking the quiet September wind.

A deep strath opens in his path. The sun has not yet risen high enough to shine upon the river which flows along the valley floor, and a pillow of mist lies about the lower hills and out over the southern end of the loch. From a long way ahead comes a call. In a moment another tern has appeared from the folds of the river cloud. Smoothly she rides into the sky. The male thrusts up to meet her.

Above the mountain's summit he catches her, pecking at her tail as she passes. Together they drop down the slopes back into the valley. Now, he decides, they really will have to move south to catch up with the flocks, or perhaps they will just fly the passage together, without the company of others of their kind. Either way they would not be lonely.

Side by side they shoot into the mist and are lost from sight. Occasionally, each time farther along the valley, a call surmounts the chuckling of the river. Many waking ears hear the voices of the terns and the sound of their wings whipping at the mist, but soon, before the sun has climbed through the mountain gap, they have gone, and nothing more disturbs the heather-land dawn.

There is one last tern, the last one in northern Scotland. He too knows that he should have left weeks earlier; but the peace of lonely shores has sapped any urge for migration he might have felt, and his strength is a fragment of what it had once been. He would not leave, now or ever again.

Movement is agony, for the twin tears where the

149

tiercel had raked him would not heal. He stands by the shore, his one good eye watching the rhythmic breathing motion of the peaty waters. The morning light, now a blaze above Ben Hope, shines against the dull feathers of his breast. His head is turned aslant and, although his senses are rapidly fading he still holds his eye to the vision of the loch.

Now the final image becomes clear. For some the great migration is over, while for others it begins again – fresh adventure, fresh danger, only the purpose is the same. A pale September sky slopes above a wild place close to the sea. Morning is woven with a washed-out light which belongs to a season almost gone, and a highland silence caresses and conceals all that has happened through the bustle of summer – and the one-eyed tern with his courage and his final sadness.

So ends *The Longest Flight*, as the last terns depart, taking their voices and their migration lust to the southernmost reaches of the Atlantic ocean. It is December and they are there now, flying through skies where the temperature is well below zero. It is probably snowing, with the wind blowing in excess of fifty miles an hour, even though high summer in Antarctica is less than a month away. Greyback, the lonely wanderer, might find those which are struggling through the terrible blizzards, and shelter them beneath his great wings; but that perhaps is only the whim of romantic imagination. Whatever the truth the silver birds will next year return when once again the northern hemisphere is tilted towards the sun. They will continue to come back to Scotland and the lands beyond until oil or our own shortsighted needs have destroyed them all, or driven them away from their ancestral home.

150

Then there will not be wild song in the sky, but only the whooping cries of sportsmen and the clanking of giant steel rigs; although even those sounds will finally fade to a lonely murmur of loss.

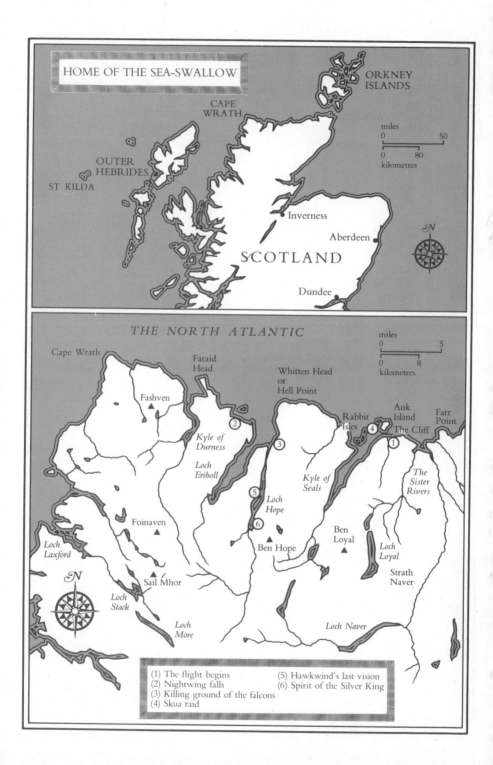

HOME OF THE SEA-SWALLOW

ORKNEY
ISLANDS

CAPE
WRATH

OUTER
HEBRIDES

ST KILDA

miles
0   50
0   80
kilometres

Inverness

Aberdeen

SCOTLAND

Dundee

N

THE NORTH ATLANTIC

miles
0   5
0   8
kilometres

Cape Wrath

Faraid
Head

Whitten Head
or
Hell Point

Rabbit
Isles

Auk
Island
The Cliff

Farr
Point

Fashven

②

Kyle of
Durness

③

④

①

Loch
Eriboll

Kyle of
Seals

The
Sister
Rivers

⑤ Loch
Hope

Foinaven

⑥

Ben Hope

Ben
Loyal

Loch
Loyal

Loch
Laxford

Strath
Naver

N

Sail Mhor

Loch
Stack

Loch
More

Loch Naver

(1) The flight begins   (5) Hawkwind's last vision
(2) Nightwing falls   (6) Spirit of the Silver King
(3) Killing ground of the falcons
(4) Skua raid